MIRANDA

MARGERY SCOTT

WHITE HEATHER PRESS

MARGERY SCOTT'S BOOKS

HISTORICAL ROMANCES

MORGANS OF ROCKY RIDGE

Travel to Rocky Ridge, Colorado and meet the Morgan men and the women who love them.

Cade

Trey

Zane

Will

Jesse

Brett

Heath

ROCKY RIDGE ROMANCE

It isn't only the Morgan men who fall in love in Rocky Ridge.

Landry's Back in Town

Substitute Bride

Wanted: The Perfect Husband

Hannah's Hero

High Stakes Bride

Jasper's Runaway

MAIL-ORDER BRIDES OF SAPPHIRE SPRINGS

Miranda

Audra

Kathryn

OTHER HISTORICAL ROMANCES

Emma's Wish

Wild Wyoming Wind

Rose: Bride of Colorado

Mail-Order Melanie

MEDICAL ROMANCES

The Surgeon's Homecoming

Stranded with the Surgeon

The Firefighter and the Lady Doc

CONTEMPORARY ROMANCES

Winterlude

*M*iranda Lowe muttered an unladylike word as the kindling tumbled down into a heap, taking the pile of coal she'd so carefully placed with it. The coal shattered on the marble hearth, crumbs exploding into the air. For some reason, today her fingers were all thumbs and she couldn't seem to build a fire even though she did it a dozen times every morning.

"Why aren't you finished lighting the fires yet?" The shrill voice echoed off the walls of the Tolliver mansion's drawing room. Mrs. Tolliver marched across the room toward Miranda. Her hawkish gaze slid down Miranda's length, her lips thinning.

"Sorry, Mrs. Tolliver," Miranda said, "I—"

Mrs. Tolliver waved a hand in dismissal. "I don't want to hear any excuses. Get them done immediately, and clean up the mess you've made, you stupid girl. I don't know why I've kept you on here for so long when you can't even set a fire properly."

Miranda's stomach clenched. She lowered her eyes. "Yes, ma'am."

"Then why are you still standing there? Get back to work!"

Mrs. Tolliver spun around and walked away, her footsteps muffled on the thick carpet.

Miranda knelt back down on the hearth to finish setting the fire in the massive stone fireplace.

"I expect all the silverware to be cleaned and the guest rooms to be done and aired out before the guests arrive as well," Mrs. Tolliver called out behind her. Then the door slammed.

Miranda sighed. This was to be her lot for the rest of her life, she supposed. The head housekeeper wasn't even close to retirement, not that she'd want the job anyway. She couldn't imagine herself ordering people around and being in charge of anything. Hadn't she been told her whole life that she wasn't pretty enough or smart enough to amount to anything?

The door opened and Lily, her best friend and one of the other maids in the Tolliver household, walked in carrying a dustmop. "Her Highness is really on the warpath this morning, isn't she?" she said after making sure no one was within earshot.

Mrs. Tolliver treated everyone as if they were peasants and she was the Queen of England. They'd given her that nickname four years before when both Lily and Miranda had come to work at the house. "As long as I stay out of her way as much as possible, the day will be much more pleasant. I'm off for four hours tomorrow."

"I don't have any time off until next week," Lily complained. "If only I could find a husband ..."

Miranda smiled at her friend. Finding a husband was as likely as finding a pot of gold at the end of the rainbow, she mused. How was it even possible to meet a man when she worked fourteen hours a day, every day except Sunday? And even then, she only got four hours off, long enough to go to church and have a short visit with her sister who lived a few blocks away.

She arranged the kindling back in the fireplace on top of the newspapers and piled the coal on top. Reaching into her apron pocket, she dug out a box of matches, then struck one and held the flame against the paper until it caught fire.

She sat back on her heels for a moment, watching as the flames licked at the kindling. Then, satisfied the fire wasn't going to go out, she got to her feet and swept up the mess she'd left on the hearth.

Suddenly, the door burst open and one of the kitchen maids rushed in. It was unusual to see any of the kitchen staff upstairs in the house. Miranda gave her a curious glance.

The maid's face was flushed, her voice panicked. "Miranda! Miranda!"

Miranda's heart jumped into her throat. "What is it? What's wrong?"

"It's Beth ..." she said, her breaths coming in loud gasps. "The baby's coming. A boy came to the door ... said to tell you to come quick."

The coal scuttle fell from Miranda's hand, clattering

on the hearth. Coal spilled out, spewing coal dust onto the floor and into the air.

Miranda scrambled to her feet, the mess forgotten. Her pulse raced, and a chill washed over her. "What's happened?"

"Don't know. He just said to hurry."

For a few moments, Miranda was frozen in place. Suddenly, she felt Lily's hands on her back. "Go," she said, giving Miranda a gentle shove toward the door. "I'll clean up the mess, and if we're lucky, Her Highness won't even realize you're gone before you're back."

"Thank you." Miranda untied her apron, pulled it over her head and half-tossed it at Lily. "I'll be back just as soon as I can."

Her shoes clicked on the marble floor as she raced through the hallways and down the stairs to the kitchen and the back door.

A light drizzle was falling when Miranda stepped outside, but she didn't want to take the time to go back to her small room on the third floor to get her umbrella. She needed to get to Beth as quickly as possible.

Miranda had taken care of Lily since their parents were killed in a carriage accident five years before. Miranda had been lucky enough to find employment in the Tolliver household and Beth had begun working in one of the factories in Beckham when she'd finished school. She'd fallen in love with the owner's son, a scoundrel who'd ruined her and left her expecting his child.

Beth had been fired from her job and Miranda had used all her savings to support her. Now, finally, the baby was coming. Soon, they'd be able to leave Beckham and build a new life somewhere far away where no one knew about the child.

Miranda ran the whole way to the rooming house where Beth lived and climbed the stairs to the third floor. A small, stout man with mutton whiskers and ruddy cheeks and a woman with a mop of frizzy white hair were standing outside Beth's door.

"Are you Miranda?" the man asked.

"I am," she replied, her breaths coming in short gasps.

"I'm Dr. Pratt. This is Elsie, the midwife."

It was then Miranda noticed the blood staining the man's shirt. Her heart began to thump wildly in her chest. "Why are you here? The midwife—"

"She sent for me. Your sister ran into some trouble delivering the child—"

"Then why aren't you inside looking after her? Is she all right? And the baby?"

"There was too much bleeding," the doctor said quietly. "I did everything I could, but it wouldn't stop. I'm sorry ..."

Miranda saw the doctor's lips moving, but the pounding of her pulse in her ears drowned out his words. The world spun, and she sank to the floor.

Two hours later, Miranda trudged down the lane behind the Tolliver house to the back door and stepped inside. If she was lucky, she could get to her room without running into Mrs. Tolliver or Miss James, the head housekeeper. She needed to change her uniform and do something with her hair before she went back to work. She had no time now to grieve. That would come later, after their work was done and she could crawl into her bed in the room she shared with Lily.

After the doctor and the midwife had left, she'd stayed and held Beth's hand until the undertaker had come and taken Beth and her baby away. The funeral would be held the next afternoon at the small church that Beth and Miranda had attended since they were born. She'd made sure Beth and her baby would be buried together. She had no idea how she'd pay for it, but the minister she'd spoken too had sympathized and had told her not to concern herself with that at the moment. She thought he'd said something about a special fund for cases like hers, but she was in such a brain fog she couldn't really remember.

She was grateful to the minister for his kindness and thankful that Beth and her child wouldn't be buried in a pauper's grave.

Miranda had almost reached the top of the stairs when Mrs. Tolliver's voice stopped her in her tracks.

She turned and looked down. Mrs. Tolliver was standing at the bottom of the stairs, her hands on her hips, her lips pressed into a hard line. "Come down here at once," she said.

Miranda knew she was in deep trouble, but surely even Mrs. Tolliver would understand why she'd left in such a hurry, and without permission.

"I'm sorry," Miranda began. "My sister—"

"I cannot have you all running off willy-nilly whenever the mood suits you."

"It was an emergency," she protested. "I would have asked permission before I left, but there was no time, and Lily said—"

"Yes, she told me your sister had an accident. How is she?"

By the bored expression on her face, it was obvious Mrs. Tolliver wasn't really interested and was only asking out of propriety. "She died," she said quietly.

"Oh ... well, my condolences."

"I didn't even get a chance to see her," Miranda went on. "I'm terribly sorry I left so suddenly, and Lily offered to—"

"I'll be speaking with Miss James about her, too. She has her own duties to perform without doing yours as well."

Even though Miranda's grief was overwhelming, guilt was building as well. Not only was she in trouble, but now her best friend would be the brunt of Miss James's anger, too. "She was trying to help. It won't happen again."

Mrs. Tolliver glared at her. "You're right. It won't. Your behavior was unacceptable. I'm relieving you of your duties here."

"What?"

"While I sympathize with your loss, I can't have people in my employ that I can't rely on, you understand."

Miranda didn't understand at all. She'd worked in the Tolliver house for four years, and this was the first time she'd ever left the house when it wasn't her scheduled time off.

"I'll speak to Miss James. Whatever is owed to you will be waiting for you in the kitchen when you've packed your things."

"But—"

"Let this be a lesson to you, Miranda. No employer will care about you or your personal problems, and if you manage to find a position in another household, it's to your advantage to remember that."

Miranda's mouth hung open as Mrs. Tolliver spun on her heel and walked away.

It didn't take long for Miranda to pack her few belongings in a worn carpetbag, and within the hour, she walked out the back door of the Tolliver house for the last time. She had no idea where she was going or how she was going to survive, but at least she had the daily newspaper Lily had slipped to her on the way out. She'd find somewhere to sit and look at the ads, and hopefully find a place to live and another job.

All she wanted to do was hide away somewhere and release the grief suffocating her, but she had no time to wallow in self-pity. If she didn't find another job today, she wouldn't have anywhere to sleep. She couldn't even go back to Beth's rooming house. The landlord had made it clear he had people waiting for a room.

She'd heard about what could happen to women who were homeless, and the thought of spending the night in an alley somewhere or sleeping on a park bench terrified her.

A short time later, she found herself wandering down Beckham's main street. The rain had stopped, and even though a few clouds remained in the sky, the sun was shining. Birds chirped in the trees, children were already back outside playing in the puddles, and people were hurrying about on their errands.

Miranda's stomach gurgled. She hadn't eaten yet since the fireplaces always had to be cleaned before she was allowed to have breakfast. When she'd heard about Beth, food had been the last thing on her mind.

She didn't have much money and she hated to spend any of it on food, but she had to eat something. Turning a corner, she stopped in at a small café and took a table in the corner.

"Morning, miss," a young woman said as she approached the table. "What can I get you?"

"A scone and a cup of tea, please."

"Right away, miss."

After the waitress left, Miranda took off her gloves and put them in her reticule, then opened the newspaper. Her heart sank when she studied the help wanted ads. She didn't qualify for even one of the positions advertised. Giving up on finding a job for the moment, she began flipping the pages, searching for a room to rent. A small ad in a box near the bottom of a page caught her eye. "Are you looking for a husband? Adventure? Security? Men out west are anxious to marry. See Miss Elizabeth Miller, 300 Rock Creek Road."

The waitress came back with her tea and scone.

"Nice and fresh," she said, setting the plate holding a warm scone and a dollop of butter in front of her. "If you need anything else, just let me know."

After the waitress moved away to take care of a new customer, Miranda sliced the scone and slathered it with butter, then took a small bite. She'd better eat slowly, since she didn't know how long it would be before she'd get another meal. She'd have to eat as little as possible to make her few coins last as long as she could.

As she sipped on her tea, she scoured the ads for a room to rent. Every room she saw advertised was more expensive than she could afford.

Her eyes drifted back to the ad for women to go west. Could she really marry a man she didn't know? She could be a good wife. She was sure of that. She was a good cook and she could clean a house and do laundry, but what man would want a woman who looked like a sheepdog, as her mother used to tell her?

Hopefully, a desperate man would. She was out of options, and it couldn't hurt to go and see Elizabeth Miller and find out if there was a man out west who wouldn't mind marrying a woman who was ... ugly.

She scanned the rest of the ads while she finished her tea and scone, hoping she'd missed something that would help her situation, but found nothing. She paid her bill and stepped outside. Rock Creek Road was only a block from the Tolliver mansion on the well-off side of town. It was only a few blocks away from where she was, and she knew if she didn't go right now, she'd likely not be able to work up the courage later. And then where would she be?

CHAPTER 2

*M*iranda stood outside the house on Rock Creek Road and took a deep breath before climbing the steps and lifting her hand to the door knocker. She wished she'd worn a dress more becoming than the drab brown one she'd put on when she left her uniform behind, but she hadn't been thinking straight.

Almost before she'd finished knocking, the door opened and a young man only a few years older than she was appeared in the entrance. He was quite handsome, and it was plain to see that he was very muscular beneath the butler's suit he was wearing. "May I help you?" he asked.

"I ... I'm here to see Miss Elizabeth Miller," she said, her voice cracking.

He opened the door wider to allow her inside. "Your name?"

"Miranda Lowe," she replied.

She had to admit she was a little surprised that he

11

didn't even ask why she wanted to see his employer, but assuming Miss Miller ran an advertisement in the newspaper frequently, she supposed women came to the door regularly.

"Please follow me." He turned and led her down a hallway toward the back of the house, then opened a door and stepped aside for her to enter.

A pretty blonde woman with green eyes looked up from the desk where she was sitting.

"Miss Miranda Lowe to see you, Miss Miller," the butler said.

"Thank you, Bernard," Miss Miller said, getting up and coming around the desk. She held out her hand. Miranda couldn't help noticing the difference between hers and Miss Miller's when she shook it. While Miranda's hands were work-roughened and callused, Miss Miller's were soft and her nails perfectly manicured.

"Bernard, could you please bring us some tea and cookies?" she asked, then turned to Miranda and smiled sweetly. "Or would you prefer coffee?"

"Tea is fine, thank you," Miranda replied. She wasn't hungry or thirsty, but she thought it wise to take whatever food was offered to her. It would save her some money she'd need later.

After Bernard left, Miss Miller gestured toward a sofa against the wall. "Please have a seat," she said. "And call me Elizabeth. May I call you Miranda?"

"Of course," Miranda said with a slight smile.

While Elizabeth returned to her desk, Miranda perched on the edge of the sofa. She set her carpetbag on the floor beside her and clasped her hands tightly in her lap. Was she really about to apply to become a mail-order bride? Elizabeth seemed to be waiting for her to speak, but she couldn't seem to form a sentence. "I'm here ... that is ..."

"You're here about the advertisement for mail-order brides, aren't you?"

Miranda nodded, suddenly feeling a bit embarrassed that she was willing to marry a stranger just so she could have a husband.

"I've helped many women find husbands," Elizabeth said. "I'm sure I can help you, too. But first, tell me why you've decided to be a mail-order bride."

Miranda's throat tightened and tears stung her eyes. Unable to hold them back, she lowered her head and dug into her reticule for a handkerchief.

Elizabeth got up and came to sit beside her. She didn't speak, but waited until Miranda was finished crying. Finally, Miranda took in a shuddery breath and sniffled back the last of her tears.

"I've worked for four years for the Tollivers over on Beacon Place," she began. "This morning, a boy came to the door to tell me my sister was having her baby and that she needed me. I shouldn't have left without asking permission, but she's the only family I have... had. I had to go to her. But I was too late. She died before I got there."

Elizabeth wrapped an arm around Miranda's shoulder. "I'm so sorry," she said softly.

"Thank you."

"What happened then?"

"After I arranged for her funeral, I went back to the

house, and Mrs. Tolliver told me she couldn't keep me on. So I have no way to earn a living now. I have nothing left here, so when I saw the advertisement, I thought it would be a good idea to go somewhere else, start over..."

"I see," Elizabeth said. "You do realize it can take some time to find the right man and to arrange for travel west."

"How long?"

"It could take two or three months."

Miranda sighed. She hadn't thought of how she'd survive until she left Beckham. "I do have some savings, but I have to pay for Beth's funeral. I've looked in the newspaper for another position but I couldn't find anything. I need to marry sooner because my money won't last months."

"I assume the Tollivers will ask you to leave," Elizabeth said. "Do you have somewhere to go?"

Miranda shook her head. "Mrs. Tolliver already made me leave," she said.

"Then you shall stay here."

"I couldn't impose—"

"Don't worry about that," Elizabeth said. "I have an empty room you're welcome to use. And I'll enjoy having the company."

"As I said, I don't have much money, but I'll gladly pay—"

Elizabeth brushed the offer aside. "If you have enough money for your personal needs, that's all that matters."

"I do."

"Good," Elizabeth said, patting Miranda's hand. "Now, let's find you a husband, preferably one who's in a hurry for a bride."

Getting up, she crossed to her desk and began to shuffle papers. "Can you cook?"

"I used to be a really good cook, but I haven't cooked much since I started working for the Tollivers."

"What did you do there?"

"I was one of the downstairs maids there, so I cleaned mostly."

"But you know how to cook?"

"My mother taught me to cook when I was growing up. Said I'd need to be a good cook to land a man since I'm not pretty and I'm too plump for any decent man to want me."

"Your mother told you that?"

Miranda nodded. "She said she was telling me for my own good."

"Then let me tell you something," Elizabeth said. "Your mother was wrong. You are very pretty. Your hair is a lovely shade, and you're not plump at all."

Miranda felt her cheeks reddening. Elizabeth was just being kind, that was all. Her sister was the pretty one, the one who had suitors calling on her night and day. A lump formed in her throat, making it hard to contradict Elizabeth. And it was nice of her to try to make her feel better.

Just then, Bernard came in carrying a tray. He set it on the table in front of the sofa and left without a word.

Elizabeth dug a piece of paper out of the pile on her desk. "Do you like children?" she asked.

Miranda loved children, but she'd given up even thinking about ever having a family of her own. After all, she'd have to be married, and since she'd never even had a suitor, marriage wasn't in her future. "I do. Very much."

Elizabeth grinned. "How do you feel about going to Texas?"

Miranda had read about Texas, about the war with Mexico and about the Texas Rangers, but she knew little else other than it was far away. "That would be fine."

"Then I think I've found the right husband for you. His name is John Weaver and he lives in Sapphire Springs, Texas," Elizabeth said, getting up and joining her on the sofa. "I'll pour the tea while you read his letter."

Miranda's fingers trembled when she took the letter from Elizabeth.

Dear Miss Miller,

My name is John Weaver, and I live in Sapphire Springs, Texas. I'm looking for a woman who's willing to marry me and to help me raise my twin five-year-old girls.

I'm 28 years old, about 6' tall and weigh about 200 pounds. I have black hair and blue eyes and I'm not the worst looking man in town, so I guess that's something. I own a diner in town and have a small house nearby.

My wife died a few months back and since then, my aunt has been helping out with the girls so I can keep the diner

*going, but she's not a young woman and it's not going
well. I think taking care of two little girls is too much for
her. They need a mother who's capable of teaching the
girls the things they need to know and I hope will eventually love them as much as I do.*

*I'm not particular about looks, but I would like a woman
who's between 20 and 25 and who can cook, since I'd
really like somebody else to fix my meals when I get home
from cooking at the diner all day.*

*If you know of a woman who's willing to work hard in
exchange for a husband who'll support her and a family
who'll treat her well, I look forward to hearing from you.*

John Weaver

"What do you think?" Elizabeth asked, setting the
tea in front of Miranda.

What *did* she think? Could she really do this? "Yes.
I'll go to Texas," she said before she could change her
mind. "What happens now?"

Elizabeth got up and went back to her desk. She
took a piece of white paper out of a drawer and put it
on top along with a pen, a bottle of ink and blotting
paper. "I have a few things to take care of," she said.
"Why don't you write a letter to Mr. Weaver and tell
him about yourself while you finish your tea? I'll be
back in a little while."

Elizabeth left the room and Miranda sat at the desk,
her mind in a whirl. What could she say about herself to

make a man—a stranger –want to make her his wife? There was no point in lying, she decided, since he'd know the truth as soon as he saw her. She began to write.

Dear Mr. Weaver,

My name is Miranda Lowe and I live in Beckham, Massachusetts.

I've been working for a wealthy family for the past few years, so I'm used to hard work. I used to be a good cook. I haven't done much cooking lately, but I don't think it would take long to come back to me. I do know how to clean, do laundry, and sew so looking after a home wouldn't be hard for me.

I'm twenty-two years old, and healthy. I have brownish-red hair that curls a lot when it's hot outside, and green eyes. I do want to be honest. I'm not pretty, so I'm glad you said looks aren't important. Also, I'm not thin, so if having a slim bride matters to you, I'm not the woman for you.

I love children and had given up the thought of having children of my own so I'd be thrilled to help you raise your girls as well as make your life as pleasant and easy as possible.

If you think I might be the kind of woman you're looking for, I'd be happy to come to Texas and marry you.

Sincerely,
Miranda Lowe

Miranda studied the words she'd written. Her heart thumped wildly in her chest. This was a drastic step that would change her life forever. She was terrified, but at the same time, a small flutter of excitement rushed through her.

She closed the bottle of ink and set it and the pen aside. She was just finishing her tea when Elizabeth came back. "Here it is," she said. "Do you want to read it first?"

"Your letter is between you and Mr. Weaver," Elizabeth replied, opening a drawer and taking out an envelope. "I'll mail it for you immediately. You should get a reply in about three weeks or so."

Miranda got up and crossed to the sofa where she'd left her reticule. "Thank you for everything, Elizabeth."

Elizabeth smiled. "I'm sure you'll be the perfect bride for Mr. Weaver. Now, why don't you go and get your things and come back? In the meantime, I'll ask Bernard to get a room ready for you."

Miranda glanced down at the worn carpetbag, shame filling her. At her age, she should have a home of her own and a family, or at least have more than two dresses and a few books to her name. "This is all I have."

"Oh, I see. Then why don't we have some lunch and get to know each other while Bernard takes your bag upstairs?"

CHAPTER 3

*J*ohn Weaver cast a quick glance at the clock on the shelf above the worktable in the diner's kitchen. Almost closing time, thank goodness.

The diner had been busier than usual all day. Probably the weather, he figured. The temperature had been hovering around ninety degrees for the last week, and folks had likely decided it was just too hot to cook. Those that could afford it had come to the diner to eat their meals. It was good for John's pocketbook, but between the heat, the lack of sleep because of the heat in the house at night, and making sure he spent time with the girls in the evenings after he closed up, he was exhausted.

The bell above the door jingled. John sighed. He'd have to tell the latest customer that he was closing when a voice called out across the diner. "Hey, John. What's the special tonight?"

Pete Fallon, John's best friend, was sliding into a

21

chair at an empty table when John opened the door separating the kitchen from the main dining room.

A smile creased John's face. "I was just about to close up."

Pete took off his hat and set it on the chair beside him. "I know, that's why I waited until now. The diner was too crowded earlier. Am I too late to get anything to eat?"

"I can rustle you up some fried chicken, mashed potatoes and beans. Cherry pie for dessert. Will that do?"

"It'll have to. I'm starved. I just hope it's better than last night's steak," Pete teased.

John approached the table with silverware and a napkin. "Didn't kill you, did it?"

"I was lucky."

John and Pete had been friends since Pete had hit him in the head with a shovel when they were four years old. Once the blood had been cleaned up, the two boys had gotten over whatever they'd been fighting about and their friendship had begun, a friendship that was even more important to John now that Nancy was gone.

Pete had been there to get him through his darkest days right after Nancy died, and Pete's mother had helped him out with his five-year-old twin girls as much as she could, considering she was getting on in years.

John had tried to hire a housekeeper, and when that didn't work out, he'd looked for someone to help him in the diner so he could take care of the girls. Not one person met his requirements.

It was then his aunt had offered to take care of the girls until he could figure out what to do.

Aunt Ruth had lived alone as far back as John could remember, but she'd barely spent any time in John's house, either before or after Nancy died.

The morning after she'd offered to help with the girls, she'd arrived full of spit and vinegar, declaring the house unfit for humans to live in and the twins out of control. She'd taken charge that day, and if the girls weren't devastated enough by losing their mother, they were even more miserable after Aunt Ruth arrived. They'd grown more unhappy by the day until he started to wonder if they'd ever recover.

His chest still tightened when he thought about the tears at the breakfast table just that morning. Ellie had climbed into his lap and put one small hand on each of his cheeks, her tear-stained face only a few inches from his, and begged him to stay home with them.

Hope, on the other hand, had glared at him through her tears, not saying a word.

He couldn't stay home with them every day, but they didn't understand that.

He'd been at his wits' end when Pete had suggested he send away for a mail-order bride. He wouldn't even consider it at first. He'd loved Nancy since the minute he'd seen her at a church social. They'd married and had the girls less than a year later. His life had been perfect.

And then, suddenly, she was gone. And he was left alone to care for two little girls and run a business.

"Any news yet?" Pete asked when John brought him a plate piled high with potatoes, chicken and corn.

John shook his head. "Maybe there isn't a woman out there who's willing to take on a ready-made family."

"My cousin out Lubbock way managed to find one, and he's got five kids."

"I hope you're right," John said with a sigh. "Things can't go on the way they are. The girls used to be normal little girls, chattering all the time, laughing..."

"They had a mother then," Pete pointed out. "You think they're going to be the same now?"

John shook his head. "Of course not. I expect them to still miss their mother, but it's been almost a year now. They should be at least getting back to their old selves instead of getting more and more miserable. Trouble is, I'm pretty sure it's my aunt's doing. She's so strict with them, but I can't complain. It's her way and she did raise her own kids, so maybe she's right. I just want to see them smile again, that's all."

The bell over the door jingled as the last customer left, giving John a wave. John went to the door, locked it and turned the sign hanging on the door to read "Closed."

He still had a mountain of dishes to wash, floors to sweep and tables to clean before he could head home. Hopefully the girls would still be awake and he could spend some time with them.

He'd check in the morning, and if there was still no reply to his letter to Elizabeth Miller, he didn't know what he'd do.

It was still early the next morning when John headed down the main street to the mercantile. Sapphire Springs didn't have a regular post office yet, just a small counter in the back of the store where the stage dropped off the mail.

"Morning, Hank," he said when he went inside. Hank Fenton looked up from the pile of letters and packages on the counter in front of him and returned the greeting. "Any mail for me?"

Hank turned his back on John and plucked out a letter from one of the slots on the wall. "Here you are," he said, handing the letter to John. "It's from Boston. You have kin back east?"

John shook his head. The only person in town who knew he'd sent for a mail-order bride was Pete. He sure wasn't about to share the information with anybody before he'd even told his aunt. The last thing he needed was for her to find out through the gossips in town before he even knew if there was a woman out there who was willing to come to Texas and marry him.

"Thanks." Tucking the letter into his pocket, he said goodbye to Hank and left the store. Already, it promised to be another scorching day, which meant the diner would be busy and he'd be run off his feet until after sundown.

He hurried down the street to the diner and unlocked the door. He should get started preparing the meals while it was still relatively cool inside, but he knew he couldn't stand to leave the letter unopened until that night.

He went inside and wove his way between the tables until he got to the kitchen, then took the envelope out of his pocket and sat down at the scarred oak table. For a few seconds, he stared at the flowing handwriting on the envelope before he opened it and took out the single sheet of paper inside.

The guilt inside him stopped his lips from lifting in a smile as he read the words. Miranda Lowe had agreed to marry him. Marrying a stranger was a gamble. He knew that, and he wasn't a gambling man. But he also knew he had to do something to try to give his girls a happy childhood, and as much as he loved his aunt, the girls would never be the smiling little girls he remembered while they were in her care.

Aunt Ruth might have raised eight of her own children, but from what he'd heard about them, none of them were what he'd call successful or happy.

So even though Miranda Lowe might not be the perfect mother, he was willing to take the chance that the girls would be happier with her. A sense of relief and anticipation filled him.

He looked up and spoke into the silence. "Nancy, honey, I got a letter today from a woman who's going to come here to be my wife and be a mama to the girls. I don't want to marry again, but the girls need a mother who'll love them, and I know you'd want them to grow up happy."

He paused, as if he expected Nancy to give him her blessing. "Her name's Miranda, and she sounds like a good woman. I'm going to send her a train ticket in the morning. It's the right thing to do, but wherever you are, I hope you know I'll always love you. That will never change."

Now all he had to do was tell his girls and Aunt Ruth.

Miranda breathed in the honeysuckle perfume and the heady scent of roses as she strolled through Elizabeth's garden. It had been almost three weeks since she'd sent her letter to John and she was impatient. She couldn't take advantage of Elizabeth's hospitality indefinitely, and even though she wasn't paying her full share, her savings were dwindling, especially after the cost of Beth's funeral.

Every morning, she scoured the newspaper, looking for a position as a chambermaid or even a cook's helper, but hadn't found anything suitable. If she didn't hear back from Mr. Weaver within the next few days, she'd have to assume he didn't want her. Then she'd have to find somewhere else to live, and some way to support herself. There was only one way she knew of, and she knew she'd rather starve.

"I thought I might find you out here." Elizabeth's voice floated on the air.

Miranda turned and smiled. "You have such a beautiful garden, I could stay out here forever."

"I enjoy it, but I don't spend as much time in it as I'd like to." Elizabeth crossed to a corner of the garden where a pair of wrought-iron chairs and a small glass-topped table sat in the shade of a large elm tree. "Come and sit down," she said. "A letter arrived from John."

Miranda's heartbeat stuttered. Could this be the letter that would change her life, or was it another rejection?

She crossed the garden and joined Elizabeth at the table. Elizabeth took the envelope out of her pocket and slid it across the table to Miranda. As Miranda reached to pick up the envelope, Elizabeth rested her hand on top of Miranda's. "I hope it's an acceptance, but don't worry if it isn't. I'm sure there's a husband out there who'd be happy to have you as his wife. And you're welcome to stay here as long as you need to. Now I'll leave you alone to read the letter. I'll be back in a few minutes and we'll talk."

Elizabeth got up and walked back to the house, leaving Miranda alone.

Her fingers trembled as she opened the envelope and withdrew a piece of paper and something else—a ticket for a train leaving Beckham to take her to Austin, Texas in two days.

Dear Miranda,

You seem like the perfect woman to make me and my girls a family again. I'm enclosing a train ticket that will bring you to Austin. I'll close the diner for the day and meet you there and bring you to Sapphire Springs, which is about two hours away. The town is small and we don't get to the city often, so I hope that's not going to be a problem for you.

If you don't mind, I'd like to get married right away. I do have to warn you that the girls are worried that you'll force them to eat vegetables and that you you'll put them to bed far too early. My aunt (who's been helping me for the past few months) doesn't approve of me remarrying, so I only ask that you be patient with her until she gets used to the idea.

I'm enclosing some money for you to buy whatever you need for your trip, and so you'll be comfortable when you get here. There's only one mercantile in town and my aunt tells me there isn't much selection of ladies' clothes. It's very hot here, so you might want to buy some thin dresses before you get here.

I'm anxious to meet you, and I'm looking forward to a wonderful life with you as my bride.

Your future husband (hopefully),
John

Miranda folded the letter and slid it back into the envelope. Her heart was galloping in her chest, and her fingers trembled. She was really going to do this! She was going to travel to a town in Texas she'd never heard of, marry a complete stranger and become a mother to two little girls.

Trepidation swirled inside her, yet she couldn't help feeling as if this was the answer to every prayer she'd ever said. Somehow, deep inside, she sensed that by going to Texas, all her dreams would come true.

Elizabeth came back as Miranda laid the envelope on the table. "Is the letter the response you hoped for?"

It was, but at the same time, it was terrifying to leave everything she'd ever known behind and go off to a strange place where she knew no one. Still, she had nothing left in Beckham, and she was convinced a fresh start would be the best thing that could happen to her. "He wants me to come to him. He sent a train ticket. It leaves in two days."

"That's not much time," Elizabeth said with a smile, "but I'm sure we can get everything organized in time. We'll go shopping in the morning."

"I don't need anything—"

"Of course you do," Elizabeth countered. "Every new bride should have something pretty to wear on her wedding day."

Miranda stood up, feeling a little shaky. "I'd hoped I'd have time to make a new dress or two, and perhaps even to sew a wedding dress." She let out a short laugh. "I can sew quite well, but even I can't make a dress in less than two days."

"I'm sure we can find a suitable dress tomorrow."

Miranda nodded. "Then it looks like it's settled. I'm leaving for Texas the day after tomorrow."

"Are you ready to leave?" Elizabeth asked two mornings later when Miranda came down the stairs from her room.

Miranda was carrying her carpetbag holding the new dress she'd bought the day before as well as all her other possessions. "I suppose I am," she replied, forcing some cheerfulness she didn't feel into her voice. After all, her whole life was going to change in a few hours.

"Good," Elizabeth said. "I'll walk with you to the station and see you off."

Miranda shook her head. "That's really not necessary," she said. "You've already done so much for me—"

Elizabeth waved away her objection and slid a glance at her watch. "Nonsense. I want to go with you."

It was a fairly short walk to the train station, and when they arrived, the two women sat together on the bench on the platform.

Miranda's heartbeat thundered inside her chest. She'd never been on a train before, and the thought of spending ten days inside the monstrous machine screeching into the station made her stomach twist into a knot. Well, that and the thought of marrying a man she'd never met.

Still, what choice did she really have?

"I made you some sandwiches for the trip," Elizabeth said, getting up and handing Elizabeth a paper bag. "They won't last long, but you'll be able to save a little money by not having to buy food today."

Miranda wanted to tell Elizabeth how grateful she

was for everything the woman had done for her, but she couldn't find the right words. "I...thank you..."

Elizabeth patted her hand. "You're very welcome," she said. "Now there is one more thing I want to say to you before you leave."

Miranda peered at her. What hadn't Elizabeth told her?

"I want you to write to me as soon as you get to Texas so I know you arrived safely."

"Oh…of course I will…"

"And then, I want you to write to me again once you're settled, maybe two weeks or a month later. Not all men are the way they appear to be in a letter," Elizabeth went on. "If you find that John isn't the man you thought he was, you're not obligated to stay with him. I don't want you to feel that you're stuck if you find yourself in a situation where you might be hurt…either physically or mentally."

Miranda nodded. "I won't."

"Good." Elizabeth smiled. "If you aren't comfortable with the situation in Texas, you need to come back immediately."

"I have nothing left here—"

"You have a friend," Elizabeth said. "Me. And if you want to come home at any time, you're welcome to stay with me for as long as it takes for you to find a job and a place to live."

"Thank you, Elizabeth. Knowing I have somewhere to go if I need to eases my mind a lot."

"All aboard!" The conductor's voice filled the small station.

The two ladies hugged. "Don't forget to write to me when you get there and let me know you're all right and that you've met John."

"I will." Tears stung Miranda's eyes. She wasn't used to such kindness. Mercy, even her own mother had never been so affectionate and worried about her.

"Now you'd better get on the train before it leaves without you." Elizabeth walked with her to the steps. A porter waited there to help her into the car.

After another quick hug, Miranda climbed the steps and found a seat inside. A few minutes later, the whistle blew. The train began to move slowly as it left the station.

Miranda looked out the window and waved to Elizabeth until she was out of sight, then settled back in the seat.

Fear and excitement filled her, although she couldn't say which she felt more. This was an adventure of a lifetime, and she was determined to be positive. She looked around as the train picked up speed and left Beckham behind. This train would be home for the next ten days.

CHAPTER 4

*J*ohn climbed out of the buggy in front of the train depot in Austin. He wanted to make a good first impression on his bride so he'd put on his Sunday clothes. It wasn't even noon yet, but with the sun already beating down, it didn't take long before he realized he'd made a mistake. Sweat beaded on his forehead and trickled down his back.

The train was a day late because of a freak summer storm, which meant he'd had an extra day to worry about the decision he'd made.

His aunt had made her disapproval of his plans clear, and with every negative comment she'd made, his worry had grown until he'd been almost ready to send a telegram to Miss Miller and cancel. But, he'd reasoned, if he did that, what would happen then?

Every day Ruth was in charge of Hope and Ellie, they grew more and more despondent. He appreciated his aunt's help and didn't want to hurt her feelings, but something had to change. If he had a new wife, there

35

wouldn't be any reason for Aunt Ruth to stay. Surely she'd see that and a confrontation could be avoided.

But what if Miranda didn't want to marry him when she got here? What if she didn't like the children, and what if the girls didn't like her? He couldn't decide which would be worse.

It was too late for worry now, though, he thought as he gazed toward the horizon and saw the smoke billowing from the train's smokestack.

He wasn't alone on the platform, but he'd bet he was the only one who was planning to marry a woman coming in on that train. A woman he'd never seen before.

All too soon, the train's wheels screeched as it slowed down. With a last belch of thick smoke, the train stopped, the doors opened and the passengers began to disembark.

He was surprised at how many people were getting off in Austin. The town had grown since the last time he'd been there three years ago. It was too big, as far as he was concerned. He liked the size of Sapphire Springs —big enough that it had a school and a doctor and a church and a mercantile. He didn't need much else. And it was still small enough that he knew his neighbors and they knew him. It did mean everybody knew everybody else's business, too, but he was all right with that. It meant that if somebody had trouble, there was always help.

He watched the people getting off the train, wondering how he would recognize Miranda. He wasn't sure exactly what she'd meant by brownish-red hair, but he figured it wasn't the dark brown hair he saw on a young woman who gave him more than a passing look as she walked by.

The depot emptied. A lone woman sat at the other end of the platform, a carpetbag at her feet. She looked lost, sad. That couldn't be Miranda, though, he said to himself.

This woman was pretty, her hair a rich coppery-gold color. A few tendrils had escaped the severe knot at her nape and framed her face in curls. And where Miranda had said she weighed too much, this woman was perfectly proportioned. He wouldn't want a woman who was stick-thin. This woman had curves in all the right places and enough meat on her bones for a man to hold onto. But overweight, definitely not.

He hoped the woman wasn't Miranda, but since they were the only two people left on the platform, it looked like she was his new bride.

He swore, but luckily he was still far enough away from her that she couldn't hear him. Where was the woman with the frizzy hair, the woman who'd led him to believe she hadn't missed many meals?

As if she sensed someone staring at her, she lifted her head and looked in his direction. Her green eyes speared him and she gave him a tentative smile as she rose and started walking toward him.

"Mr. Weaver?" she asked in a voice barely more than a whisper.

"You're Miranda?" He hadn't meant to sound so surprised, and felt a little guilty that he hadn't hidden it better.

Her cheeks pinked and she lowered her gaze. "I...am."

He swore again.

Miranda's eyes widened at the muttered curse that slipped from her future husband's lips. Was he the kind to swear often? She hoped not. She supposed many women lied about their appearance in their letters. She'd told the truth, so she hadn't expected him to be surprised that she looked exactly the way she'd described herself. He didn't have to make his disappointment quite that clear.

She wasn't beautiful. She wasn't slim. She wasn't any of the things that turned men's heads. And as if that wasn't enough, after ten days on a train, she was a mess. After all, she hadn't been able to do more than wash herself with a cloth and a basinful of tepid water since she'd left Beckham. Her hair held the dust of...how many miles had she traveled anyway?

"Sorry, ma'am, that slipped out," Mr. Weaver said.

"I understand I'm not what you hoped for, but I did warn you—"

"No, it's not that," he began.

She waited, expecting him to tell her exactly what his problem was if it wasn't her appearance.

"Never mind," he went on. "I'll deal with it. Is this all your luggage?"

She nodded.

He picked up the carpetbag. "You travel light," he

commented. "I sent money for you to buy some new things so I expected you to have a trunk at least. Why didn't you spend the money I sent?"

"I did spend some," she replied. She'd bought a few toiletries, one dress to be married in and gifts for the twins, but she still had most of the money he'd sent in her reticule. She'd return it to him once they reached Sapphire Springs. "I thought it might be better to wait until I got here to see what I'd need since it's you said it's so much warmer here," she replied. "Which it is," she added with a smile, fanning herself.

"I'm told the mercantile doesn't have much selection."

"I'm sure there's plenty," she said. "After all, the other ladies in town manage, don't they?"

"I suppose they do…"

"As long as my clothes are practical, I'm satisfied. I may need to buy a thin dress if mine are too warm, but that's all."

He smiled. "You can buy more than one. I'm not rich, but I do earn enough in the diner that you and the girls don't have to do without the necessities."

She gave him a smile. "I don't need much, so I promise I won't drive you into the poorhouse."

He grinned. "I can't ask for more than that. The wagon's over there. We'd better get going. It'll take us about two hours to get to Sapphire Springs, and I expect you'll want a little time to prepare for the wedding."

"That would be wonderful. In fact, I'd love to take a bath if there's time."

"The wedding's set for four o'clock," he said. "I

thought you might want to take a bath after being on the train for so long, so I arranged for one to be ready for you when we get there."

She was surprised he was so thoughtful. Only one other man she'd ever known had been kind, and that was her father. The only other men she'd really known were the Tolliver men, and kindness wasn't something they knew anything about.

Surely a man who would think about his bride's comfort was a man who would be kind in other ways as well.

"How was your trip?" he asked after he'd helped her into the wagon and they were on their way to Sapphire Springs.

"Long," she said with a grin, "but interesting. This country really is so beautiful and I did enjoy the journey. I do admit I'll be happy to lie down in a real bed tonight, though." When her brain caught up with her mouth, she felt herself blush. Heavens, what must he think of her even mentioning a bed. Would he think she was anxious for the wedding night? "Oh...I apologize...what I mean is..."

He slid a glance in her direction, his eyes twinkling. "There's no reason to be shy. We're going to be married by tonight and I hope we can be comfortable enough with each other to talk about anything we want to, even beds."

She nodded slightly to show him she agreed, even though she couldn't imagine ever being anything but embarrassed to talk about some things.

"The bed might not be the most comfortable bed

you've ever slept in," he went on, "but I can guarantee it won't be moving."

She giggled. "That will be quite a change after so long on the train."

They drove in silence for a few minutes. The sun beat down, and Miranda couldn't remember ever being so hot. Summers in Beckham could get hot, too, but not like this. Now she understood what he'd meant about wearing thin clothes. She'd have to make a trip to the mercantile as soon as she could.

Trying to take her mind off the perspiration trickling down her back, Miranda studied the flowers blanketing the fields as far as the eye could see. "What kind of flowers are those?" she asked. "I've never seen them before."

"I'm not sure," he told her. "but they bloom every year at this time. I think they only grow in Texas, too."

"Do they grow in Sapphire Springs?"

He nodded. "Outside of town."

"Lovely. The Tollivers always had fresh flowers in the house. They brightened the rooms and made them feel very welcoming. I'll pick some for your house if you don't mind."

He looked at her, his expression serious. "It's going to be our house," he pointed out. "You can do whatever you want to so that you feel at home there."

Miranda felt very lucky that she'd found a man who seemed to be eager to make their marriage a good one.

"I'm curious." John's voice filtered into her thoughts. "Why did you decide to become a mail-order bride? Surely you had offers to marry from men back east."

She shook her head. "Not one."

"I find that hard to believe," he said with a grin.

Miranda shifted in her seat to face him. "It's the truth," she said. "I was in service to a wealthy family. I worked at least fourteen hours every day except Sunday."

"You only got Sunday off?"

She let out a short laugh. "Heavens no, we didn't get the whole day off. We were allowed four hours on Sundays, enough time to go to church and to take care of any personal needs. We got an entire day off once a month."

A frown creased his forehead. "That doesn't seem right."

"It isn't, but work was hard to find, and if I wasn't willing, there were plenty of other girls who'd be happy to have a roof over their heads and food in their stomachs. So you see, there really wasn't time for courting at all."

"So you decided to write to me?"

"Not exactly," she replied. "I expected to live the rest of my life in service. My sister was expecting a baby. One day I got word that the baby was coming. I left the house without permission. When I got to my sister's rooming house, I found out both she and the baby had died. I hoped I could get back to the Tollivers' house without anyone knowing I'd been gone, but when I returned, Mrs. Tolliver was waiting for me. She told me to leave immediately. I had nowhere to go, no family left, and very little money. I saw the advertisement and went to see Miss Miller. She showed me your letter so I decided to write."

"Where did you live until you left to come here? What did you do?"

"While I waited for your response, Miss Miller was kind enough to allow me to stay with her until your letter came." She smiled. "And here I am."

"I'm sorry for your loss," John said. "So you have no family left now?"

She shook her head.

"I'm glad you came to me. At least you understand what the girls and I are dealing with." He reached over and squeezed her hand.

His touch sent a wave of sensation up Miranda's arm and through her entire body. No man had ever touched her before, and her heart began to race. Was this what it would feel like for any man to take her hand, or was it just John's touch that made her react this way?

She so wished she could ask Lily. Maybe she'd know, although she couldn't remember Lily ever mentioning a suitor either. Neither of them had had time for any life outside the Tolliver house. Once she was settled, though, she'd write to Lily and ask her.

I do understand," Miranda told him. "My parents were killed when I was fifteen, and even at that age, it was so hard to cope with. I can't imagine how those poor little girls must be hurting right now. How do they feel about you marrying again? Are they worried about having a new mama?"

"To be honest, I'm not sure," he said. "It's been almost a year now, but they don't seem to be healing. In fact, they seem sadder now than they were in the beginning."

"That's strange," she said. "Time usually does help to heal, especially in young children."

"I hate to say it but I think it might have something to do with my aunt."

Miranda's brows arched. "Your aunt? How?"

He gave her a wry smile. "Let's just say she's...strict. She believes in routine, in firm discipline and that children should be kept busy. Idle hands, you know?"

"I don't know much about children. Perhaps she's right."

"Nancy…that was my wife's name…Nancy and I believed in discipline, too, but not to the extent Aunt Ruth does. Were your parents strict?"

"They were, but in some ways, I was lucky. My sister and I had responsibilities and chores, but we also had freedom to be children. I explored the woods behind our house, I swam in the river, I played games with the other children I knew."

"What about your sister? Didn't she play too?"

Miranda chuckled. "Heavens, no. Beth didn't like to get dirty. She preferred to stay inside with Mother and sew and read."

"That sounds like Hope and Ellie. Different as night and day."

The drove in silence for a few more minutes before he spoke again. "Were you and your sister close?"

Miranda's throat tightened and tears welled up inside her, but she tamped them down. "We were. Even though we were so different, she was my best friend. My mother lamented the fact that I wasn't more like her, though. I couldn't be the lady Mother wanted me to be."

Miranda realized she'd said more than she'd intended. She couldn't tell him that she'd grown up always being second best, how her sister's fragile beauty and small stature had always made Miranda feel inferior, about how her mother had always pointed out how lacking she was and that no man would ever want her because she wasn't pretty or the right size.

"It doesn't sound like you had a very happy childhood."

She didn't want his pity. "Oh..." She let out a laugh that sounded brittle to her ears. "I only meant that my childhood wasn't perfect, nothing more. I do, however, believe it's the responsibility of the parents to make it as perfect as possible for their children. And that includes fun, and making sure the children know they're loved unconditionally."

His smile faded, and she wondered if she'd said something wrong. "Of course, if you prefer a stricter routine—"

"No," he interrupted. "For a second or two, you just reminded me of Nancy."

Something in the tone of his voice told Miranda that the reminder wasn't something he was happy about.

He'd made a huge mistake in sending for a bride, John thought, casting a quick look at the woman beside him

45

in the wagon. She was far too pretty, and the second he'd taken her hand in sympathy, desire had surged through him, a sensation he'd never expected to feel again.

Miranda was going to be his wife. She was going to live with him, and lie beside him every night for the rest of their lives. He'd never love another woman the way he'd loved Nancy, but Miranda seemed like a good woman. There was no reason they couldn't have a good marriage.

His heart would always belong to Nancy, but it would be so much easier to remember that if Miranda wasn't so pretty. And so…nice.

At the same time, he wanted a woman who was nice, who would grow to love his children as much as he did, and would care for them and teach them. He shrugged inwardly, realizing it was impossible to have both.

His thoughts consumed him as they traveled the well-worn trail between Sapphire Springs and Austin.

"I was hoping your children would be with you when you came to meet the train so I could start getting to know them." Miranda's voice filled the silence.

A slow smile lifted his lips. "I did plan to bring them with me and they wanted to come, but Aunt Ruth thought it would be best for them to stay at home where they could stick to their routine. Four hours or so is a long time for them to sit still in a wagon."

"That's true," she agreed. "I'm sure I'll be anxious myself to move around by the time we reach town, so for a child, it would be doubly difficult. I'm sorry I don't know more about children, but I'm eager to learn and I promise I'll be the best mother I can be."

He turned to smile at her. That was all he could ask. "I'm sure you'll be a wonderful mother."

"So they're with your aunt now?" she asked.

He nodded. "She'll keep them until tomorrow so we can have tonight to ourselves."

She turned away, but not before he noticed her cheeks flush again. He admitted to himself that he found her modesty appealing, and he wondered if she was as innocent about the intimacies between men and women as she appeared to be.

"I'm looking forward to meeting them," she said. "What are they like?"

"They look exactly the same and they're so close it's like they're two halves of the same person, but ..." He chuckled, then continued. "On the inside, they're different as night and day. They've changed since their mother died, though. They're sadder now, quieter, and they don't really take an interest in anything. Hope is so quiet that sometimes it's as if she isn't even there."

"I'm sorry, I don't know anything about raising children, but I do want to help them," Miranda said.

"I think you'll do just fine," John commented. "Ellie has started to come around a little, but she's not the same happy-go-lucky little girl she was before. Of course, Aunt Ruth makes it hard for her to be that girl."

"That's understandable after a loss like that," Miranda put in.

"Ellie used to be outgoing and loved being around people, well, she was until her mother died. She wore her heart on her sleeve, and whatever she was feeling, everybody around her knew about it. She's not like that now, though. Hope, on the other hand, has always been a bit quieter, a bit shy. She tends to hold her feelings in until she feels comfortable with strangers. But they both loved to be busy and do new things. I hope one day they'll feel that way again, especially now that you're here."

"I'll do my best."

He looked at her then, saw the sincerity in her green eyes. A sense of calm washed over him. Everything was going to be all right.

Well, except for the fact that he was attracted to the woman who was going to be his wife, and the fact that he was already starting to like her more than he wanted to.

CHAPTER 5

*M*iranda's heart thumped in her ribs as she waited at the back of the church for John's friend, Pete, to return from telling the minister and John that they were ready. John had sent Pete to bring her to the church, and as she'd climbed the steps into the church, she'd asked him to walk her down the aisle since she had no one. She really didn't want to face strangers alone.

She'd never been comfortable being looked at, and especially since these people were John's friends. She could imagine the whispered words of criticism behind their hands.

"Ready?" Pete asked, tucking her hand into the crook of her elbow. "The music's about to start."

Her legs were trembling so badly she was afraid she'd fall down and make a fool of herself. Focusing on putting one foot in front of the other, she let Pete lead her down the aisle, her eyes fixed on the stained glass window above the altar.

She didn't even look at John until she stood in front of the minister and John took her hand. He smiled down at her and she pasted a smile on her lips. The preacher's words faded as her mind drifted to the man standing beside her, the man who was going to be her husband within a few minutes.

He was so much more handsome than she'd expected. He'd said in his letter he wasn't the ugliest man in town, but she was sure there were very few men in town, if any, who could hold a candle to him.

His hair, black as coal, glistened in the rainbow of light coming through the window. Although it was short, which she assumed was proper as the owner of an establishment where food was served, it curled at the ends, and a few curls tended to dip down his forehead.

But it was his smile that made her heartbeat stutter, his voice that sent a tingle through her when he spoke to her.

Suddenly she realized all eyes were on her. Her face flamed.

John leaned closer and whispered to her. "This is where you say you do. At least I hope you're going to say you do."

"Oh... yes..." She turned to the preacher. "I do."

The preacher grinned, and a few seconds later, he pronounced them husband and wife and gave John permission to kiss her.

Her breath caught in her throat. She'd never been kissed before, and to have her first kiss be in front of so many strangers made her feel positively weak.

Her gaze locked on his as he cupped her chin and lowered his face to hers. His lips gently brushed against hers, yet the effect was as if he'd branded her. She'd never felt such an intoxicating sensation before, a sudden urge to be closer, to press her lips against his...

Suddenly, he drew away, a frown creasing his forehead as he gazed down at her parted lips. Had the kiss been so terrible for him? Perhaps since he'd been married before, he had expectations she didn't know about.

A moment later, his smile was back and the preacher introduced them as Mr. And Mrs. Weaver.

Miranda stood quietly beside John as a tall thin woman and two little girls rose from the front pew and approached them. He crouched, gathered the girls into his arms and bussed their cheeks. Then he got to his feet he introduced her to his aunt.

"I'm happy to meet you, Mrs. Edmonds," Miranda said, offering her hand.

"Ruth is fine," she replied. Miranda had been around enough of the Tollivers' friends to recognize the disparaging tone in her voice. It seemed John was oblivious, though.

Keeping his arms around the girls' shoulders, he looked down at one of them. "This is Ellie," he said. Shifting his gaze, he added, "and this is Hope."

Ellie gave her a hesitant smile, while Hope held back, sliding out of the curve of her father's arm and hiding behind him.

The girls were adorable, both with hair the color of

cornsilk, eyes wide and bright blue. She wondered if she'd ever be able to tell them apart, at least by appearance.

Emotion tugged at Miranda's heart. Immediately, she knew it would be so easy to love these children as her own.

Ellie took a step toward her and gazed up at her with pursed lips and frown lines appearing between her brows. "Are you our new mama?"

"I am," Miranda said, giving her a wide smile. "Is that all right with you?"

She didn't answer for a few seconds, then nodded. "Why do you got brown spots on your nose?"

Miranda saw Hope's lips quirk in a tiny smile. She was about to explain to Ellie that the spots were freckles when Ruth's sharp voice interrupted. "Ellie! Don't be rude!"

Hope's smile disappeared. Ellie jumped, startled. Fear filled her eyes.

It was plain to see that the girls were afraid of their aunt. So this was why John had decided to marry. She didn't blame him one bit.

Ellie's head lowered. "Sorry," she said quietly.

Miranda wanted to take Ellie in her arms and assure her she wasn't offended. She also wanted to tell John's aunt that Ellie's question was a perfectly normal one, but she didn't think it would be wise to interfere in how Ruth cared for the girls, at least not yet. She'd never had children, so she had no experience in dealing with discipline, and by the expression on Ruth's face, she suspected the woman would be quick to point that out. "It's all right," she said gently to Ellie. "Why don't we talk about it tomorrow?"

Ellie nodded. "Okay."

"Come along, girls. You can see your father later." Ruth whisked the twins away. Soon Miranda and John were surrounded by well-wishers and it was impossible to think about anything except memorizing names and who was related to whom. Did John know absolutely everybody in town?

It seemed to take forever, but finally, the crowd thinned out. "They're heading to the hotel for our wedding supper," John told her as he ushered her out of the church and along the boardwalk toward a three-story brick building near the center of town.

"We're having a wedding supper?" she asked, surprised. She'd expected that their first meal together would be with his family.

He nodded. "I was going to cook myself but a few of my friends wouldn't hear of it. They were determined we should have a proper wedding supper and then they proceeded to invite everybody in town."

"Oh...well...that was very nice of them..." She couldn't imagine anyone she knew..0 well, except for Lily...taking on extra work to do something special for her. The people in town must think highly of John, she reasoned. Warmth stole over her.

John chuckled. "Everybody loves a celebration, so whenever there's a good excuse, you can count on everybody pitching in to make it happen. You must be hungry by now, so we'll stay long enough for you to eat and then we'll go home. How does that sound?"

Miranda had been so nervous she hadn't thought about food, but now that he mentioned it, she realized she wasn't just hungry, she was starving. As if her stomach wanted to emphasize it, it rumbled. Loudly.

Mortified that he'd heard the gurgling sound, her eyes flew open. He was laughing, the deep timbre of his voice sending a warm tingle through her. Tiny laugh lines appeared in the corners of his eyes, and even though her face felt hot, she let out a giggle. "I do like to eat," she said with a grin.

He wrapped her hand in his. "Then let's hurry before all the food is gone."

"You don't look happy, my friend," Pete said, coming to stand beside John at one of the tables in the hotel dining room while Miranda chatted with two of the ladies who'd helped organize the supper.

John had been pleasantly shocked when they'd entered the hotel dining room. The owner, Josiah Ferguson, had closed off the dining room to everybody except the wedding guests. Tables laden down with food lined the walls of the room, and small tables covered with white tablecloths dotted the space. One longer table was set apart, and the owner had told him that it was reserved for John and his bride.

"I'm fine," John replied. "Been a long day is all."

"Sure is a surprise to me that you found yourself another woman who'd put up with you. But then, you were smart enough to find a woman who doesn't know you."

John sent his friend a withering glance. "Guess that's why you don't have a wife yet. You're not smart enough to find one that doesn't know you."

Pete chuckled. "She sure is a lot prettier than you thought, isn't she? It's a good thing, otherwise I hate to think what any children you have would look like if they took after you."

A twinge of jealousy stabbed John. If Pete wasn't such a good friend, he'd be irritated that he was commenting on his wife, even if it was a compliment. In this case, though, he knew Pete didn't mean anything by it, and even though he hated to agree, he had no choice.

"I hope you're ready to move on, else it's not fair to the lady to let her think you're going to have a real marriage."

John had been thinking about that very thing. When he'd written the letter for a mail-order bride, he'd intended to have a strictly hands-off marriage. Now, he realized he didn't want that at all, and it bothered him more than he wanted to admit that he found Miranda desirable.

When he'd kissed her after the wedding, he'd been sure he wouldn't feel anything for her. The sudden need that had surged through him had been unexpected, and unwanted.

But he hadn't been able to stop thinking about it

since, and if he was being completely honest, he wanted her. All of her. Wanted her in his bed. Wanted to kiss her again, wanted to feel her skin beneath his fingers, wanted to bury himself in her warmth and watch her eyes glaze over with passion.

Making love to Miranda would be a huge risk, he told himself. He didn't want to grow close to her, didn't want to like her too much, didn't want to risk falling in love again.

But even worse, what kind of man was he to even think about betraying Nancy's memory? He'd made a promise to her, a promise he'd fully intended to keep until a few hours ago.

He didn't know Miranda yet, but something deep inside him had stirred to life the minute he'd seen her at the depot. He sensed that unless she wasn't really the woman she appeared to be on the surface, it would be easy to grow to care about her, and one day, to love her.

He'd given his word to Nancy, and he didn't ever go back on his word. But did he really want to live the rest of his life without love?

For the next hour, Miranda tasted dishes much like those she'd cooked in Beckham, but some she'd never seen before. The Mexican foods she tasted were spicier than what she was used to, and her body heated, but she couldn't be sure whether it was from the food, from the way John's thigh kept brushing against hers, or the way he leaned close to her and whispered in her ear several times during the meal.

She'd met so many people, too. She knew she'd never remember all the names, but a few ladies had made an impression—Rosita Juarez's exotic beauty, Poppy Aldridge, with the slender frame that reminded Miranda so much of Beth, and Freida Swansen with her pale blonde hair.

The women were friends themselves, and within a few minutes of the introductions, they had invited Miranda to join their quilting bee. Miranda was adequate with a needle and thread, but didn't have the expertise she was sure they expected. Still, she was thrilled to be included, happy that she was being accepted as John's wife and a new resident in town.

Finally, Miranda and John said goodnight to the guests and exited the hotel. Dusk had fallen, and the blistering heat of the day had cooled. Still, it was warm and pleasant.

John took Miranda's hand and strolled slowly down the boardwalk and around a corner. She admitted she liked the feel of his hand wrapped around hers.

"This is home," he said, stopping in front of a two-story house set back from the dirt road. "It's not very big but I can add to it if we need to in the future."

Miranda's nerves tightened. The only reason they would need to add to the house would be if they had children. And in order to have children, she'd have to allow John to... Her face flamed at the mere thought of what he could—and had every right to—do to her now. She'd heard about the marriage act from a friend, about how painful it was and how it was a wife's duty to submit to her husband as often as necessary, to try to think about something else until he was satisfied no matter how unpleasant it was.

"What's wrong, Miranda?" John's voice interrupted her thoughts. "You look flushed. Are you sick? Did something you ate not agree with you?"

She looked up at him, saw the concern in his eyes. "Oh...no...it's nothing..." She pasted a grin on her face. "Nothing at all."

"Are you sure? I can go get the doctor—"

She rested her hand on his arm. "I'm fine." She turned away from him and walked up to the house. "The house is lovely, John," she said. And she meant it. Flowers lined the stone path leading to a large front porch. "I can't wait to sit out here in the evenings."

He smiled at her and opened the front door. Suddenly, he scooped her up in his arms. She let out a squeak and without a thought, wrapped her arms around his neck and hung on. "What are you doing?"

"I'm carrying you over the threshold," he said. "Do you mind?"

She couldn't answer. Her only thought was that he must have the strength of Samson to be able to pick her up as if she weighed no more than a bag of feathers. That he would even want to pick her up was a surprise. "No," she said finally as he carried her into the house and kicked the door shut behind him. "I don't mind at all."

She'd never felt a man's arms around her, and she

58

had to admit it felt nice. When he carefully set her back on her feet, she was even a little disappointed.

The house was quiet. "When will your aunt and the girls be home?" she asked.

"They're not coming home tonight. They're staying at my aunt's house so that we have one night alone."

"Oh... that's right. You did tell me that before, didn't you?" How could she have forgotten that she'd be alone with John for the entire night?

"This is our wedding night, after all."

She couldn't speak, her voice stuck in her throat.

"I'll show you the rest of the house, then I'll go sit on the porch and give you some time to get ready for bed before I come in. Is that all right with you?"

She nodded.

"Like I said, the house is small but it'll have to do for now," he said, taking her hand again. "You can see this is the parlor."

The room was small, but cozy. Miranda didn't see a speck of dust anywhere. The room was so perfect that it was hard to believe anyone even lived in the house, especially children.

A brightly colored hooked rug lay on the plank floor. A settee sat against one wall and two stuffed armchairs flanked a stone fireplace. A piano took up space on the wall beside the door to the kitchen. A music book was propped open. "Do you play the piano?" she asked.

John shook his head. "Nancy played. She'd always planned to teach the girls, but..." His voice trailed off, and she regretted bringing up a subject that obviously caused him pain.

"The kitchen is through here." John guided her through an open door. Just like the parlor, the kitchen was immaculate. A large cookstove sat against one wall. A counter lined the rest of the wall, and an oak table with six chairs filled the center.

Miranda crossed to a large cabinet on the opposite wall. She opened the door and saw it was filled with supplies and dishes.

It made sense that his kitchen would be well-stocked, she supposed. After all, he did own a diner, so food was important to him.

"If there's anything else you need in here, just let me know."

"I will," she replied. She'd been a good cook once, and she'd particularly loved to bake. She was going to enjoy working in such an organized kitchen.

"The bedrooms are upstairs. There are three, but one is empty. When I built the house, Nancy and I expected the girls would each want their own room, but when we tried to separate them, they got so upset we decided to leave them together."

Was he going to give her the empty room? Maybe she'd been worrying about nothing. She felt the tension ease a little until he took her upstairs. "This is the girls' room," he said, opening the door to another room that showed no signs of life.

"The room at the end of the hall is empty, and this is ours," he said, turning and opening a door directly across the hall from the girls' room.

Ours! She'd been wrong. He intended for them to share a room.

"There's space in the wardrobe and two drawers in the bureau for your things."

"Thank you," she replied.

"I'll go now," he said, "but if you need anything, I'll be right outside on the porch."

She nodded, her body trembling. She'd never been so terrified in her life.

CHAPTER 6

Miranda heard John's footsteps fade as he went down the stairs. The front door opened and closed behind him, and she was left to stare at the bed occupying the center of the room.

She didn't know how long he'd be outside, so she quickly undressed. She caught a glimpse of her reflection in the mirror once she'd removed her corsets. She let out a resigned sigh. If only she was slim like Beth... She only hoped John wouldn't be too disgusted by her.

She heard the front door close. Should she get into bed, or wait for him? She wasn't sure, but as the sound of his footsteps grew louder, she made a decision and climbed into bed.

It was still warm outside, but she pulled the quilt up to her neck.

Her heart raced, and her stomach twisted as the door opened. He stepped into the room and closed the door behind him.

"I was worried I didn't give you enough time," he

said, crossing the room and sitting on the edge of the bed to take off his boots and socks.

"I had time," she croaked past the dryness in her throat.

"Good. Once you're more comfortable with me, you won't need privacy."

Miranda couldn't imagine ever undressing in front of a man, even if he was her husband. But she didn't want to argue, so she kept quiet and watched as he stood up and tugged his shirt loose from his pants. She couldn't tear her gaze away from the muscles rippling beneath his skin when he slid the shirt off. Then he unbuttoned his pants and kicked them aside, leaving him in just his drawers.

He got into bed and turned down the lamp. The bed shifted under his weight as he rolled to his side to face her, then propped himself up on one elbow. "Would you mind if I kiss you again?"

The memory of his lips on hers after the wedding sent a tingle through her. She shook her head.

His fingers gently grazed her cheek then his hand slid behind her neck to cup her head while he lowered his lips to hers. He brushed his lips across hers, tracing the seam of her lips with his tongue.

Miranda wasn't sure if she was supposed to do something, but as the kiss deepened and the pressure of his tongue grew firmer, she parted her lips, hoping that was what he wanted. His tongue immediately slid into her mouth.

A soft moan escaped her lips as his tongue found hers and tangled with it, sending sparks of heat through her veins and igniting a need for... something... low in her core.

The sensations coursing through her body were indescribable, and she never wanted them to end.

John's hand released her, his fingers tracing the curve of her jaw. His hand lowered to her waist, then slowly moved to cup her full breast through her nightgown.

She sucked in a gasp as his thumb grazed her nipple. Surely this was wrong. This couldn't be part of relations, could it? Nobody had ever mentioned anything like this. Not that it was unpleasant. If she was being honest with herself, she liked it. His touch sent a delicious sensation through her, and she couldn't help hoping he'd do the same to her other breast. She had an urge to shift slightly to make it easier for him to gain access. Did that make her wanton? At the moment, she didn't know, and she didn't really care.

Suddenly, he drew away and flopped onto his back on the bed, his breathing ragged. "I'm sorry. I know we're married, but this can't be part of it."

A chill washed over her. Her worst fear had come true. He'd touched her and he'd been repulsed. Her throat tightened, and she rolled over to face the wall. "I understand," she said past the lump in her throat. "Goodnight."

Dawn hadn't yet broken when Miranda got out of bed and quickly slipped into her clothes. She'd lain awake all night, listening to the sounds of the night and gazing at

John's profile in the moonlight streaming through the lace curtains at the window.

She'd been terrified of marital relations, but she knew they were part of marriage for a man. From what she'd heard—which wasn't much, she'd admit—every man wanted to couple with a woman. And no matter how she tried to excuse him, it was clear. He didn't want *her!*

Well, she decided, they could still have a good marriage. They could be friends, and if that was the only kind of marriage she could have, she could be content with that. Couldn't she?

Quietly, she made her way downstairs and lit the lamps in the kitchen. John would be cooking all day, so she wanted to make him a nice breakfast before he left.

She opened the cabinets lining the wall, her mood lifting when she saw the well-stocked shelves. She would have no trouble coming up with a meal in this house and couldn't wait to cook all the dishes she used to love. For this morning, she needed something simple since she didn't know what time he'd be leaving for the diner. She only hoped John liked the French toast she planned to make.

The cookstove lit easily, and she left it to heat while she found a skillet and butter. She'd noticed a basket of eggs on the counter. She found a bowl and cracked eggs into it, adding a little milk and whisking the mixture until it was blended and frothy. She'd seen a loaf of bread on the shelf, so she hunted through a drawer until she found a knife and sliced the bread into thick slices, then dipped them into the egg mixture until the bread soaked up the egg.

Letting the butter melt in the skillet first, she added the bread, letting it cook and brown on both sides, then placed each slice in a long baking pan.

She'd noticed a jar of peaches on the shelf which would be perfect to add to the French toast. Draining some of the juice, she spread the peaches on the French toast, sprinkled cinnamon and nutmeg on top and set the pan in the oven to keep warm while she set the table.

"Good morning."

John's gruff voice startled her. She spun around and met his gaze, a tingle rushing through her. His black hair was tousled and his eyes were still heavy from sleep. Stubble shadowed his chin, and for some reason, she had an urge to feel it beneath her fingers. "Good morning."

He looked tired, and she couldn't help wondering if he'd slept as badly as she had.

For a second or two, she wondered if he would mention what had happened between them the night before. But he didn't.

He crossed the kitchen and took a mug down off the shelf, then poured himself a cup of coffee. "What are you making?" he asked. "Something smells good."

"I thought you might enjoy a meal you didn't have to cook yourself."

He grinned. "I would."

"Then sit down and I'll serve," she said, picking up a towel to wrap her hands while she took the baking pan out of the oven. She slid a spatula under two pieces of

French toast and spooned some of the remaining peaches on top, then set it in front of him.

"What do you call that?" John asked, sliding into one of the chairs at the table.

"French toast."

"I've never heard of it."

"The Tollivers—the people I worked for—used to travel to Europe frequently. They came back and asked their cook to start making it. There are a lot of variations, some with fruit, some stuffed with vegetables, some plain with maple syrup. When I had any spare time, which wasn't often, I used to help in the kitchen."

John sliced a piece of the French toast and stabbed it with his fork, smothering it with the peaches and brought it to his mouth. He let out a groan of satisfaction as he took his first bite.

"I'd better be careful. If you keep cooking like that and word gets out, folks will want to eat here instead of my diner," he said with a grin.

"I'm glad you like it." Miranda poured herself a cup of coffee and began to eat her own meal. They ate in silence, and when they were finished, she got up and started clearing the table. "Is there anything in particular you'd like for supper?"

"No," he said. "I'll just be grateful not to have to cook it myself. Now, how about if I show you the diner before Aunt Ruth brings the girls home?"

"Are you not going to work today?"

He shook his head. "I'm closed today. I thought it would be nice if we could spend a day together with the girls so they get used to you before I left them again."

Miranda's respect for him grew. He was a man who thought of others before himself, and before money, two things she wasn't used to.

"So, would you like to see it?" he asked again.

"I'd love to," she replied. "I would like to clean up here first, though."

"I'll help," he said, coming to stand beside her. He picked up a dish cloth and slid his hands into the water she'd heated earlier. "I'm pretty good at washing dishes. I've had lots of practice."

Miranda brought the other plates to the sink. "I'll let you help, but only because I'm eager to see your diner. After that, you are no longer welcome in my kitchen except to eat."

"What about if I want to kiss you again?" he asked.

Miranda's heartbeat skittered in her chest, the question such a surprise she dropped the plates. Luckily they landed in the water, sending up a shower of soap suds. "Oh..."

John grabbed a towel and wiped his face. He turned to face her, a grin creasing his lips. "Is that a yes or a no?"

An hour later, John and Miranda walked down the boardwalk toward The Blue Sapphire. *Their diner*, John had corrected her earlier when they'd left the house and she'd expressed her eagerness to see it. She doubted she'd ever be able to think of the diner as theirs, but she appreciated that he was willing to share everything he had with her.

Finally, John stopped in front of a long building. The exterior had been painted white, the shutters and door sapphire blue. Fitting, she thought, in a town called Sapphire Springs.

While Miranda waited, John unlocked the door. A bell jangled when he opened the door and stepped aside.

The diner was small, but welcoming. Eight tables covered with white tablecloths dotted the main dining area. A vase filled with flowers—wilted now, she noticed—decorated each of the tables. Lamps dangled from ornate hooks at intervals around the space, and a multi-faceted crystal chandelier hung from the ceiling. "Oh, John," Miranda exclaimed, stopping just inside the door. "It's lovely. I expected..."

"What?"

She didn't want to tell him she'd expected a rustic room with a few mismatched tables and chairs. She definitely hadn't expected anything this elegant. "It's really lovely, John," she said. "It seems much smaller than it looks on the outside."

"This is only half of the building. The other half is empty," he told her. "It was originally a saloon, but when the original owner died, his son closed the saloon and divided the building into two. I bought this half three years ago. I'd like to buy the other half and expand one day, but I expect it'll get sold before I can come up with the money."

"How much do you need?" she asked. Not that she could help him. She had no money of her own.

He named a figure that stunned her. She couldn't imagine ever saving that much money.

"I'm proud of it," he said. "I've worked hard and it's paying off. It's full most every night, and folks seem to like the food."

Miranda could see the pride on his face and hear it in his voice. It filled her with joy, and she hoped that somehow she could help him realize his dream. "Is the kitchen through there?"

He nodded, then followed her as she wove her way through the tables and opened a door at the back of the building.

A huge kitchen greeted her—two cookstoves, a large icebox, shelves holding ingredients, and a long counter that ran through the center of the room. It was much larger than the kitchen in the Tollivers' house, and there were often four or five women bustling around preparing meals there at any one time. "Once you expand, you won't even need to enlarge this kitchen," she commented.

"I know," he agreed. "I planned it that way."

"Very smart." Her respect for her new husband rose a few more notches. Not only was he handsome and easy to get along with, he was proving himself to be a shrewd businessman with a plan for the future.

"Anything you'd like to know about it?"

"Not right now. I'm only sorry you had to close the diner because of me. It really wasn't necessary—"

"I didn't close *because* of you. I wanted to close

because I wanted to spend a little time getting to know you and to show you around before I left you to deal with the house and the children."

"I appreciate it, but you've lost income because of it. Is there some way I can help you to make up for it?"

He shook his head. "No, but thanks for the offer. Knowing the girls are taken care of and I can come home to a nice home and a good meal is all I need to help me focus on the diner. Now don't give it another thought."

"All right."

"Now, are you ready to go back home?" he asked. "I'm sure Aunt Ruth will be bringing the girls home soon. Did I tell you that she offered to still come to the house every morning and stay with you to help you take care of the girls?"

It upset her that John didn't trust her to look after his children properly, but at the same time it was under-standable. She didn't know anything about children and naturally he wouldn't want to take any chances with their safety. If anything happened to those two precious little girls because of her, not only would John never forgive her, she'd never forgive herself.

She had no logical reason why, but in their short meeting right after the wedding, she felt uncomfortable in Ruth's presence, almost like a child on the brink of being scolded. She couldn't say anything to John, though. He'd think she was being silly, and she likely was.

She'd have to put a smile on her face and accept Ruth's help, at least temporarily. Summer would be over soon and the children would be going to school, so there would be no reason for Ruth to spend her days in their house. All she had to do was get along with the woman until then.

And once the children were in school, she'd have extra time. She could work in the diner and make John's work a little lighter. Her thoughts drifted, and soon she was coming up with a plan to help John realize his dream.

CHAPTER 7

*J*ohn couldn't figure out why it was so important to him that Miranda approve of his diner. He'd never been one to worry about what other people thought. If he had, he wouldn't cook for a living. Woman's work, a lot of people thought, but most folks who wanted to eat at a diner didn't really care who did the cooking as long as it tasted good.

He was proud of what he'd accomplished, and for some reason, he wanted Miranda to be proud of him. How could that have happened in only one day?

He was sitting at the desk in the parlor working on the diner accounts later that afternoon when the front door opened and Ruth walked in. The twins followed behind, their faces serious until they saw John.

Hope and Ellie raced past Aunt Ruth, almost mowing her down in their rush to reach him. His heart swelled with love as they climbed into his lap, throwing their arms around him and snuggling tight.

75

"We missed you, Papa. Didn't we, Hope?" Ellie's high-pitched voice filled the room.

Aunt Ruth's face pursed. "Ellie, there's no need to screech like a wounded animal."

"Yes, ma'am." Ellie's smile disappeared, but she didn't budge from John's lap.

"It's all right, Aunt Ruth," John put in. "They're children. They get excited."

"That's no reason to act like savages."

"That's true," John said. "Have you had lunch?"

"We have," Aunt Ruth replied.

"Where's the lady?" Hope asked shyly, her gaze scanning the room.

"I do believe she's baking cookies in the kitchen. If you'd like to go see her, I think there might be one or two waiting for you."

Ellie bounded out of John's lap and headed to the kitchen. Hope trailed behind, her steps slower than her sister's.

"Really, John? Cookies? Children should be fed a proper diet."

A few seconds later, the girls came back into the room, each of them holding a large cookie. Miranda followed behind them. Her face was flushed from the heat of the oven and a few curls had escaped the knot at her nape.

Heat that had nothing to do with the cookies baking in the hot oven spread through him. She really was beautiful in an understated way. She'd mentioned in her letter that she was overweight. He didn't think so at all.

He looked on as Miranda smiled at his aunt, but he noticed the smile didn't reach her eyes.

"I'm sorry. I didn't think a treat now and then was going to hurt them," Miranda said, her voice holding a hint of nervousness.

"Well, far be it for me to criticize," Aunt Ruth said, "I'm sure you know more than I do about raising children," she said.

"No, I don't..."

Ruth crossed the room and rested her hand on Miranda's. "That's right. You don't. And if you don't listen to those who do, you'll raise them to be women who won't know their place or how to act like ladies. And then what man will want them?"

What man will want them? Hadn't she heard some variation of those words from her mother, day after day as she grew up? Of course, her mother had added the fact that Miranda was too fat, and not as pretty as Beth. When she was finished, she'd always added 'I suppose you can't make a silk purse out of a sow's ear' with a sigh.

No, she didn't know how to raise children, but she knew one thing—Ruth was going to make Hope and Ellie feel they weren't good enough, that they weren't pretty enough, or that their whole purpose in life was to catch a man.

She gave Ruth a sweet smile. "I promise I'll do everything I can to raise the girls to know everything they need to know."

As the afternoon wore on, John noticed the girls growing more and more withdrawn. When they spoke, it was in response to a question, their voices barely more than whispers.

He also saw Miranda glancing at the grandfather clock in the corner of the room, stifling a sigh.

Suddenly, she bounded out of the chair. "I'll be right back." Then she hurried out of the room.

John heard her footsteps on the stairs, and less than a minute later, she returned carrying two small packages wrapped in brown paper. She handed one to each of the girls. "I brought you something."

Both girls looked to John for his approval to open the gifts. When he nodded slightly, Ellie tore into hers, squealing with delight when she discovered the baby doll inside. Hope carefully untied the string and unfolded the paper carefully, a slow smile lifting her lips when she picked up her baby doll and cradled it in her arms.

"Thank you for the present," both girls said in unison.

Miranda crouched down to their level. "I hope you like them."

"I do," Ellie said brightly.

Hope nodded.

"They're yours to take care of," Miranda said with a soft smile. "But first you each have to give your doll a name."

"I do?" Hope asked, her small forehead creasing in a frown.

"Of course," Miranda replied. "You have a name, don't you?"

"Uh huh..."

"I'm sure your baby doll would like one too."

"I s'pose. You giving your doll a name, Ellie?"

"Sure," Ellie replied. "Her name's going to be Rapunzel, like in the storybook Mama used to read to us. You should call yours Cinderella."

Hope pursed her lips and shook her head. "No. Cinderella had to do chores. My doll will be Snow White."

"Okay. Let's take them to our room."

Both girls rushed out, their footsteps light. The door banged shut behind them.

"You didn't have to do that, Miranda," John said.

Miranda smiled. "I wanted to bring them something. I thought it might make it a little easier since I was a stranger coming into their lives. When I was a little girl, my dolls were...oh, never mind."

"That was a nice thing to do." He smiled at her, his dark eyes meeting hers. Her heart did a pitter-patter behind her ribs. The sensation was strange, but quite pleasant.

Ellie came back into the room and crossed to stand in front of Miranda. "We want to make them a bed. Can you come help us?"

Miranda smiled, her heart swelling. This was a start. She gave John a questioning glance. "I'd love to, if your papa doesn't mind."

John grinned. "I don't mind at all."

Miranda rose and followed Ellie out of the room. As she reached the stairs, she heard Ruth's voice. "I'm sure she means well, John, and I don't mean to interfere,"

Ruth began, "but it's not wise to spoil children. Children need to learn to work for what they want, not have everything handed to them on a silver platter."

"It's one gift," John protested. "I don't think that's spoiling them, and I'm sure Miranda didn't mean any harm."

"Well, they're your children," Aunt Ruth went on. "If you want them to grow up without any sense of responsibility, that's up to you. Now I must be going. I need to rest. The girls have worn me out with their incessant chatter. I'll be back in the morning."

"Thanks, Aunt Ruth," John said, "but it's really not necessary if the girls tire you too much. Miranda's here now—"

"And if yesterday and today were any indication, she really needs someone to teach her how children should be raised."

"I—"

"I'll see you tomorrow."

John watched her leave, then sank back into the chair and heaved a sigh. He'd noticed the way Miranda had avoided Ruth's eyes and the way she'd twisted the plain gold band on her finger when his aunt had criticized the gifts. And he was fairly sure she'd heard Aunt Ruth's comments about the cookies. No wonder she was anxious to go with the girls.

This was not working out at all the way he'd expected.

Guilt filled Miranda. She had meant well. She'd hoped a small gift would make it a little easier for the children to accept her. And for a few minutes, she'd thought she was making progress. She'd even seen a half-smile on Hope's face when she'd chosen a cookie from the baking tray.

How could she ever learn to take care of the children properly? It seemed everything she'd done so far was wrong. Her mother's words popped into her brain. "Honestly, Miranda, you can't be trusted to do anything right, can you?" How many times had she heard those words? It seemed she was still useless.

The door slammed just as Ellie tugged on Miranda's dress. "Are you coming?"

Miranda looked down into Ellie's anxious face, her heart sinking. What if Ruth was right and she wasn't capable of looking after the girls by herself? John already didn't want a real marriage, and if she couldn't be a good mother, he wouldn't have any reason not to send her back to Beckham.

Her throat tightened and tears stung her eyes. Somehow, in one day, she'd grown to care about these two little girls. And she was very quickly growing to care for their father, too.

Miranda plastered a smile on her face and let Ellie draw her into the bedroom she and Hope shared. Hope was already sitting cross-legged on the floor, her doll cradled in her arms. She looked up as Miranda and Ellie came in.

Ellie sat down beside Hope. Hope whispered something to Ellie, and then Ellie looked up at Miranda. "Can you make dresses for our dolls, too?" she asked.

"I'd love to. Maybe one day soon we can go to the mercantile and pick out some fabric for them," she replied. "Would you like that?"

Both girls nodded in unison. "But can you help us make a bed for them now?"

Miranda lowered herself to the floor and sat facing the girls. She glanced around the room, searching for something she could transform into a doll bed. "What do you think we should use?"

Just then, John appeared in the open doorway and leaned against the jamb. "You girls having a good time?"

Miranda looked up and met John's gaze.

"We are. I heard the front door close. Did your aunt leave?"

He nodded.

Was it her imagination, or did she actually see the tension ease from the girls' faces? "We're just trying to decide what to use for a bed for Rapunzel and Snow White."

John looked toward the ceiling, then a grin spread across his face. "I have the perfect bed for your dolls. I'll be right back."

He disappeared. "What is it?" Ellie called out. No answer. She shifted as if she was going to get up.

Miranda put a hand on her arm. "I think it's a surprise. You do like surprises, don't you?"

Ellie nodded.

"Then we have to be patient and wait to see what your papa brings back."

They didn't have to wait long. A few minutes later

John came back, an empty bushel basket in his arms. "Will this do?"

Miranda smiled up at him. She'd never known a man who was so involved with his children, especially daughters. Her respect for him hitched up another notch.

Ellie clapped her hands in delight, and even Hope got up to help Ellie take the basket from him and carry it across the room where they set it under the window. A frown creased her forehead. "They need covers."

"They do," Miranda agreed, "but it's very warm right now, isn't it?"

Hope nodded, but didn't speak. "They'll need one when it gets cold."

Miranda got up and took a pillow from the top of the wardrobe. "They will," she said, "and I'll make one for them before winter. What about this pillow for them to sleep on?"

The girls nodded.

Miranda tucked the pillow into the basket and flattened it.

Hope and Ellie laid both dolls on the pillow.

Miranda turned to John. "Do you have a thin towel we could borrow?"

"Sure do." He disappeared again and came back with a towel so thin it wouldn't dry a flea.

"Perfect." She tucked the towel around the dolls. "There you are," she said. "They'll be snug as bugs there until I can sew a real blanket to keep them warm in the winter."

Ellie giggled at Miranda's reference to insects. For a

split second, Miranda thought she might have seen Hope's lips twitch, but the tiny movement was gone so quickly she was sure she must have imagined it.

Miranda got to her feet as gracefully as she could since she'd noticed John watching her, a strange expression on his face. His gaze lowered from her face to her breasts, her hips, her legs. His eyes seemed to darken. His jaw tightened. Did he find her unsightly? Was he sorry he'd married her?

"What time's supper?" he asked, his voice suddenly gruff.

"It'll be ready in a few minutes," she replied. "I'll go and set the table right now."

Straightening to her full height, she moved to the door, her shoulder brushing against his chest as she passed him. She thought she heard him suck in a breath but she couldn't be sure.

Her throat tightened. How was she going to spend the rest of her life with a man who could barely stand to look at her?

John closed the iron cemetery gate and trudged down the hill toward home. The sun hovered above the mountains, casting a golden-orange glow across the sky. A soft breeze rustled the tall grass under his feet.

He'd been so sure marrying again was the answer. A mother for his children. A woman to take care of his home. He'd wanted friendship with his wife, a companion. He hadn't expected anything else. He especially didn't expect to feel a shiver of desire run through him whenever he looked at her. He didn't expect to like hearing her soft breathing as she slept beside him, to feel her warmth, to feel his skin tingle if she accidentally brushed against him or touched him during the night.

It had been less than a week, but it was getting harder and harder to keep his hands off his new bride. It was only by remembering his vow to Nancy that he'd been able to control the urge he had to wrap his arms around Miranda and carry her off to bed.

He could tamp down his desire, but what was even worse was that he liked her. She was easy to get along with, laughed easily and treated the girls as if they were her own.

It would be so easy to fall in love with Miranda, if he could let go of the memories and the promises he'd made. But he couldn't do that. He couldn't break his promise to Nancy.

Even though Miranda seemed capable of taking care of the house and looking after the girls, Aunt Ruth still arrived every morning, her grim expression telling him she wasn't pleased with whatever Miranda was doing. To Miranda's credit, she hadn't said a word whenever criticism came her way. In fact, she seemed to expect it, and let Aunt Ruth have her way.

But something had to change. And soon. He knew that. He just didn't know how to tell Aunt Ruth without hurting her feelings. She'd been a godsend when he'd needed her most, and he sure didn't want her to feel as if he'd used her and now that he didn't need her, he wanted rid of her.

The tinkle of piano keys reached his ears through the open window as he opened the gate and walked up the path to the house. A lump formed in his throat as memories washed over him. Nancy had been an accomplished pianist, and he'd spent many evenings relaxing in an easy chair, reading while Nancy played.

But those days were gone, and whoever was playing the piano had very little skill.

Swallowing thickly, he opened the door and stepped inside, his heart lurching at the sight before him.

Miranda was sitting on the piano bench, one of the girls on each side of her. Hope's fingers were on the piano keys, and as Miranda pointed to a key, Hope pressed it. Miranda was smiling at her. And Hope was smiling back!

He almost staggered from the force of emotion surging through him. He'd thought he'd never see a real smile on his little girl's face again.

"Papa!" Ellie climbed down from the bench and raced across the room, launching herself into his arms. "We was playing the piano," she told him, her eyes bright with excitement.

"I see that," he replied.

"Hope's better than me though," she went on, her smile fading. "I made more mistakes."

Miranda gave him a look that told him to be careful what he said in response.

"I make lots of mistakes, too," he said, bussing Ellie's cheek. "And you know what? It doesn't matter if you make mistakes. Do you like to play the piano?"

Ellie nodded. "Yep."

"Then don't worry about the mistakes. And maybe if you ask nicely, your mama will teach you more when she has time."

Ellie wriggled in John's arms until she could face Miranda. "Will you? Pleeeeaaase?"

Miranda grinned. "I'd love to."

John's insides lurched with emotion.

"What about you, Hope? Would you like to learn to play the piano more, too?" John asked.

Hope nodded, a shy smile on her lips.

In only a few days, Miranda had worked wonders with Hope. Another few days and maybe, just maybe, he'd have the daughters back that he thought he'd lost forever.

CHAPTER 8

*O*ver the next few days, life began to fall into a
pattern. Miranda cooked breakfast every
morning for John and the girls before he left for the
diner. Every night, while John worked on the accounts
for the diner, Miranda either played games with the
girls, taught them to play the piano or read to them.
And when she and John went to bed, he kissed her
goodnight.

Miranda was almost happy. She loved the girls like
she'd given them life, and she was falling more and more
in love with John every day. Other than the physical part
of marriage, he was everything a woman could ask for
—kind, considerate, generous. He worked hard, laughed
easily and seemed to be happy, too.

There was only one fly in the ointment—Ruth.

Every morning, she arrived shortly after John left,
and took over...everything.

No matter what Miranda did, Ruth either criticized

the way she did it or took over and did it herself. One morning, she'd even caught Ruth rearranging the clean clothes she'd hung on the clothesline. Miranda was tempted to say something, but decided against it. She'd only end up feeling as if she was wrong, and she was tired of always feeling inferior and unworthy.

At least Hope and Ellie seemed to be happy with her, she thought as she rolled out pastry for the pie she planned to bake for dessert. Realizing she'd forgotten to ask the girls whether they wanted apple or cherry pie, she wiped her hands on her apron and headed up the stairs.

As she approached the bedroom, she heard Ruth's sharp voice. "That's not the way I showed you, Hope," she was saying. "The corners must be tucked in like this. Now do it again."

Miranda stepped into the room. Hope was standing at the foot of her bed, her face a mask of misery, tears drying on her cheeks. "Is there a problem, Ruth?"

Ruth's gaze shifted from Hope to Miranda. "Not at all," she replied. "I was just showing Hope how to do square corners. You do know how to make a bed using square corners, don't you?"

"Of course I do," Miranda said. "Not when I was five years old, I admit."

"It's never too early to teach children how things should be done properly."

Miranda disagreed, just as she disagreed with many of the woman's child-rearing beliefs, but she kept quiet. Ruth was John's aunt, and she didn't want to come between them. Instead of contradicting her, she turned her attention back to Hope. "Hope?" she asked. "Where's Ellie?"

"She went...outside..." Hope hiccupped.

"Please go and find her and wait for me on the porch," Miranda said, then smiled sweetly at Ruth. "I've decided to take the girls to see their father at the diner."

Ruth's face twisted in a frown. "They haven't finished their chores yet—"

"An unmade bed isn't the end of the world, is it?"

"Cleanliness—"

"I know, but I'm taking the children out. We'll be back later."

Before Ruth could protest any further, Miranda hurried downstairs. The pie could wait. Helping the children to escape John's aunt couldn't.

The Blue Sapphire was crowded when Miranda and the children walked in. The twins were greeted by almost every one of the customers, and Miranda felt self-conscious. She did recognize some of the people since they'd been at her wedding supper, but she couldn't put names to them.

She found John in the kitchen stirring a large pot on the stove. He looked up and gave them a wide smile. "What brings you down here? Everything all right?"

Miranda nodded. The kitchen was unbearably hot and he was busy. She wouldn't add to his problems by complaining about Ruth. "We're on our way to the mercantile and the post office. I have a letter to mail to my friend, Lily, back in Beckham. I thought we'd stop in and say hello. I hope you don't mind."

"Not at all," he replied. "I'm always happy to see my three favorite ladies."

"We's gonna buy fabric." Ellie looked up at Miranda, her eyes wide. "Did I say that right?"

"Perfectly," Miranda replied.

"Mama said she'd make a blanket for Rapunzel's bed."

"Snow White, too," Hope put in.

Miranda laughed. "Yes, I did. I'd also like to buy some fabric to make myself a dress or two and some for the girls if that's all right. They're going back to school soon and I noticed their dresses are getting very tight and short."

"There's money in the coffee can on the top shelf over there," John said.

"Thank you." Miranda lifted the can down and took out a few bills. "I won't spend anymore than necessary."

John set the spoon down and turned to face her. His hands gripped her shoulders, the heat searing her and sending a now-familiar tingle rushing through her. "Miranda, I'm not poor. You don't have to scrimp. I want you and the girls to have what you need, so don't ever think I'm going to be upset if you spend money."

"I want you to save for the expansion—"

"The expansion will come, or it won't. I won't deprive my family to make that happen. Okay?"

Miranda nodded. "Okay."

"Can we go now?" Hope's voice filled the space.

"Yes, Hope, we can go now," Miranda replied with a smile.

After saying goodbye, they exited the diner and strolled down the boardwalk toward the mercantile.

All the while, an idea was forming in Miranda's brain, an idea that could perhaps help John to realize his dream sooner rather than later.

It was Saturday, and the diner was closed. It was closed on Sundays until after church, but when Nancy died, he'd started closing one day a week as well. He needed a day to spend with the girls, and he figured they needed a day with him, too. It also gave them all a break from Aunt Ruth, although he'd never admit that to anybody.

John leaned back in his chair after their noon meal and let out a satisfied sigh. "That was the best steak pie I've ever had, Miranda. I've never had pastry so light and fluffy."

"Thank you," she said softly as she got up and began to clear the table.

He noticed the tinge of color on her cheeks, and it still surprised him that compliments embarrassed her. Most of the women he'd known enjoyed flattery, but it seemed to make Miranda uncomfortable. He'd have to make a point of giving her more compliments so she'd get used to it, he decided.

Miranda had been particularly quiet all morning, and even though she'd assured him she was fine, he couldn't help worrying that something was wrong. Was she sick? And if she wasn't, did she regret marrying him? Was Aunt Ruth making her life so miserable she was thinking about leaving?

"Mama?" Hope's voice speaking to Miranda interrupted his thoughts.

Miranda smiled at Hope, who was waiting patiently for a piece of the cake and custard Miranda was serving into a bowl. "Yes?"

She pointed to a spot on her nose. "I got a brown spot like yours."

Miranda leaned closer and grinned. "You do," she said.

"Will I get lots of spots like yours?"

Miranda put the knife on the plate and smiled down at Hope. "They're called freckles," she said. "Isn't that a funny word?"

Ellie giggled.

"I don't know if you'll get lots or just one, but it doesn't matter—"

"Aunt Ruth says they stop ladies from being pretty."

"What?" John was stunned that his aunt would say such a thing.

"But you're real pretty. Isn't she, Ellie?" Hope said.

Ellie bobbed her head vigorously.

Miranda seemed to be speechless. "Your mama is very pretty," John put in. "And especially her freckles."

To prove his point, he got up and rounded the table to where Miranda was sitting. He took her hands and pulled her to her feet.

He saw the confusion in her eyes, and he understood

it. Other than their kisses before bed, he'd made a point of not showing her any physical affection. He couldn't afford to let his body betray him into breaking his promise to Nancy.

It was important to show his girls that they shouldn't be worried about a few freckles. And if he was being truthful, he thought Miranda's freckles only made her prettier. She wasn't classically beautiful, but her wide smile and bright eyes gave her an inner light that warmed his insides.

"You like her freckles, Papa?" Ellie asked.

He grinned at Miranda. "I do." Still holding her hands, he drew her toward him and lowered his head to hers. He pressed his lips gently against the freckles on her nose.

He heard her suck in a breath and pulled back a few inches. Her eyes were wide, her lips parted as if they were waiting for him to take possession.

Lord help him, he wanted to, and he probably would have if giggles coming from the two little girls at the table hadn't invaded his brain.

Releasing Miranda, he took a step back, his gaze never leaving hers. A tiny frown appeared between her brows and her teeth nibbled at her lips.

"I...I have work to do..." he said, his voice deep and gruff. Turning away, he crossed the room and went outside, not even bothering to close the door behind him.

~

John was unusually quiet the rest of the day, and when he kissed Miranda goodnight that night, he didn't wrap his arms around her as he usually did, only grazed her lips and rolled away from her. She had no idea what had caused the sudden change, and it bothered her that she might have unknowingly done or said something to deserve it.

By the time he left for the diner the next morning, Miranda had already decided the problem was the kiss they'd shared the day before. He'd regretted it. There was nothing else she could think of why his mood had altered so suddenly. They'd been having a pleasant meal until then. But what was so different about that kiss than their goodnight kisses?

Was it because it was daylight? In front of Hope and Ellie? Because there was no reason for the kiss?

She was still pondering John's sudden mood change when she glanced at the clock and realized how late it was and Ruth still hadn't arrived.

Perhaps she'd just overslept. There was no point in worrying until she had good reason. Still, it wasn't like her to be late.

A twinge of concern picked at Miranda. Had something happened to her? Was she ill? Hurt? She lived alone, so if something had happened to her, it was quite possible no one would know.

It was so tempting to just enjoy a day alone with the girls, but if Ruth had a problem and Miranda ignored it, she'd never forgive herself.

She glanced at the clock and made a decision. If

Ruth hadn't arrived by noon, she'd take the girls and walk to her house to check on her.

Meanwhile, she wanted to do something special with the girls. She'd have to hurry to finish her chores later, but it would be worth it. And she knew just what to do.

Hurrying to the bottom of the stairs, she called out to the girls in their bedroom. "Hope? Ellie? Come downstairs, please."

She heard their footsteps a few moments before they raced down the stairs and stopped in front of her. They looked up at her hesitantly. "Are we in trouble?"

Miranda chuckled. "No. Not at all. I wanted to see if you'd like to have a bricnic this morning?"

"What's a bricnic?" Ellie asked.

"It's like a picnic but they're usually in the afternoon. Since it's still morning, it can be a bricnic – after breakfast but before lunch."

"That's a funny word," Hope said. "Where will we go?"

"Just in the yard, but we'll have snacks, and you can play with your dolls. Or I can read more of *The Little Mermaid* to you."

"Yes, please," they said in unison.

A few minutes later, Miranda and the girls left the house and spread a blanket under a willow tree in the yard. She'd made lemonade and soon they were munching on scones and honey.

Ellie picked up the worn copy of *The Little Mermaid*. "Will you read to us now?" she asked, wiping her sticky fingers on a napkin and scrubbing it on her face.

"I will."

Shaded by the willow, the temperature was warm, and a soft breeze perfumed by the rose bushes along the side of the house filled the air. The girls sat cross-legged on the blanket, Snow White and Rapunzel cradled in their arms, and Miranda began to read the story of a mermaid who fell in love with a prince and after many obstacles, lived happily ever after with him on land.

Miranda had always loved the story, and she was happy to share it with the girls, hoping they'd love it as much as she did.

"Did you always know how to read?" Ellie asked. "I'm going to school soon and I'll learn, too."

"Me too," Hope added.

"I didn't always know how, but once I learned to read, I always liked to. Books can let you travel around the word and take you on exciting adventures."

And help you to hide from the reality of your life, she could have added, but stopped herself. Books had been her escape as a child, and she'd spent hours living through the characters between the pages. One of her favorites had been *The Ugly Duckling*, and she'd waited, expecting to be transformed into a beautiful woman when she grew up just as the ugly duckling had grown into a beautiful swan. She'd been disappointed when it hadn't happened, but she was old enough by then to realize it was a fairy tale and not reality.

"...and the prince—"

"What's going on here?" The voice from behind startled Miranda. She spun around and faced Ruth, towering over her and the children, her lips pressed in a thin line, her hands on her hips.

Miranda's heartbeat stuttered, and for a few moments she felt like a little girl who'd misbehaved. But she wasn't. She was a grown woman who had the right to do as she liked.

Taking in a calming breath, she smiled sweetly. "We're reading."

"Mama is telling us a story about the mermaid—"

Miranda was about to make an excuse, but stopped herself. She'd done nothing wrong. She hadn't hurt them, and they'd been happy all morning—until now.

She refused to argue with Ruth, especially in front of the children. She got to her feet. "I'll be right back," she said to the girls and moved away.

Ruth followed.

"Really, Miranda. You're teaching the girls that play comes before their chores."

"Sometimes a break in routine is a good thing. They'll do their chores later."

They need to be learning to clean, and sew and do laundry, not waste their time with their heads in books, daydreaming."

"Daydreaming? Perhaps, but they're also learning," Miranda countered. "Books can teach them about the world and everything in it without ever leaving home."

"The house needs a good cleaning—"

Miranda bristled. If there was one thing Miranda knew how to do it was clean, and she resented Ruth's thinly veiled insults.

"We'll talk about this later," Miranda said as calmly as she could manage, even though she had no intention of talking about it at all. Then, turning her back on Ruth, she went back to where the girls were waiting.

She sat down, picked up the book and smiled at them. Out of the corner of her eye, she saw Ruth storming up the porch steps. The door slammed behind her as she went into the house. "Now," Miranda said, "where were we?"

CHAPTER 9

*J*ohn closed the bedroom door behind him and crossed quietly to the chair Miranda had moved to the corner of the room. He sat down and tugged off his boots, doing his best not to wake Miranda. Not that she woke easily, he thought with a smile. She could likely sleep through a gunfight.

His gaze shifted to the bed where she'd already fallen asleep. She was lying on her side facing the middle of the bed. She'd braided her hair, but strands had escaped, curling around her face. Her long eyelashes rested on her creamy cheeks and her lips were parted slightly.

And he wanted her. Lord help him, he wanted to make love to his wife. Desire heated his blood, settling low.

Shucking off his clothes, he climbed into bed and rolled onto his side to face her. Her dark lashes rested on her cheeks. He watched as her lips curved into a soft smile. Hell, he could lie here and just look at he for hours.

Her nightgown had twisted, the neckline lowering until he could see the swell of her breasts. The fabric strained against them, and desire pooled deep inside.

He laughed inwardly. He could probably make love to her and she wouldn't even know it.

Suddenly, a cry from the girls' bedroom split the air.

Before he had a chance to even roll over and get out of bed, Miranda had already bounded up and was racing out the door.

How had that happened? How could she have heard it when she slept so soundly? He followed quickly to find Hope wrapped in Miranda's arms, tears streaming down her cheeks. Ellie was still asleep, curled into a ball, only the top of her head peeking out from under the covers.

"Hope just had a bad dream," Miranda said to John. "She'll be fine. Won't you, sweetie?"

Hope sniffled back a few tears and nodded.

"John, you go on back to bed, I'll be there in a bit."

John nodded, leaving Miranda with Hope.

As he trudged back to bed, he realized Miranda had really become their mother. That she'd grown so close to the children and that she loved them so much amazed him. Miranda was exactly the kind of woman he wanted to raise his children.

She was also exactly the kind of woman who could sneak past his defenses and make him love again. And even though he'd been fighting against it since the minute he saw her, he was losing the battle.

He was falling in love with Miranda. How was it possible to love two women? He still loved Nancy. He would love her until the day he died.

Maybe it was loneliness, and lust. Nothing more. He'd been telling himself that for the past few days, but even as he tried to convince himself his feelings for Miranda weren't love, he knew what love felt like. He recognized the loneliness he felt when they were apart, the contentment when they were together, and the need for physical contact.

He had no right to feel this way. He'd made a promise, and he'd always been a man of his word. How could he break that promise and still look at himself with pride?

Something was preying on John's mind. Miranda could sense it even though John still kissed her goodnight, still spent as much time as he could with the girls and was polite and friendly toward her.

She was tempted to ask, but at the same time, perhaps it was best if she didn't know. What if he regretted their marriage? What if he no longer wanted her?

Shaking off the feeling, she hurried through her chores, staying out of Ruth's way as much as possible.

Hope and Ellie had gone to have lunch with friends of John's and their children, so Miranda decided to go and have lunch at the diner.

Every table was occupied when she opened the door to the diner a few minutes later. She smiled at several people she recognized as she made her way to the kitchen. As she opened the door with one hand, she plucked the pin out of her hat with the other.

John needed help. How he'd managed so long by himself, she didn't know, but it did explain why he came home bone-tired at the end of the day.

She had nothing else she had to do for a few hours, so what better way to spend her afternoon than helping her husband. And just spending time with him, she added to herself.

She never tired of being with him. Even when they weren't having a conversation, their silence was comfortable and calm.

John looked up from the stove as she entered, giving her a smile. Her stomach fluttered. It was ridiculous that one smile from him could cause such a reaction inside her, but she was growing used to it.

"What are you doing here?" he asked.

"The girls are with the Andersons, so I decided to come and visit," she said, returning his smile. "Is it always so crowded at this time of day?"

He nodded, turning back to stir the contents of a large pot on the stove. "Every day."

"John," a deep voice called out. "More coffee, please?"

"Be there in a minute," John replied.

Miranda grabbed a towel hanging on a hook near the stove and picked up the coffee pot. "I'll do it."

With one hand supporting the coffee pot and one

hand on the handle, she shouldered the door open and went into the dining room. As the door closed behind her, she paused. She had no idea who'd asked for coffee. She stood, her brows creased as she squinted, searching for someone with an empty cup.

A hand suddenly shot into the air. "Over here."

With a smile, she hurried across to the table. Three young women and one older man she suspected were Hispanic were finishing their meals.

"You are John's new bride?" the man asked. An accent tinged his words.

"I am," Miranda replied. "My name is Miranda."

"Let me introduce myself," he went on. "I am Hector Delacruz and these are my daughters, Ariana, Juliana and Luciana."

The women nodded and smiled when he introduced them.

"It is good John has help now and his babies have a new mother. I raised my daughters after their mother passed, and it was not easy."

"I'm sure it wasn't."

"Can we get more coffee over here?" another voice called out.

"It's a pleasure to meet you all," Miranda said. "Now if you'll excuse me ..."

"Of course."

Miranda spun around and crossed and refilled more coffee cups. Soon the pot was empty and she headed back to the kitchen where John was spooning stew into bowls on a tray.

"I'll take them if you point out who they're for." she offered.

"Are you sure? You don't have to work here. You have enough work at home."

"I'm happy to help." She wanted to add that she wanted to be with him, even if they weren't talking or in the same room.

For the next two hours, she served food, cleaned tables and washed dishes. Finally, the diner was empty and Miranda carried the last of the dirty dishes into the kitchen and slid them into the soapy water in the basin.

Her focus on cleaning the plate in her hands, she didn't noticed John coming up beside her. He took her hands out of the dishwater and enfolded them in a towel.

He was so close she could see his pulse in his neck, feel his coffee-laced breath brushing against her cheek. "I appreciate your help, but you've done enough," he said, his gaze meeting hers. "If you have free time, you should do something you enjoy."

Her heart skittered behind her ribs as she gazed up at him. "I enjoy being with you." Heat rose in her cheeks at her forward behavior, but it didn't seem to bother him.

"I feel the same way."

Her throat tightened as he lowered his face toward her. He didn't usually kiss her during the day, and even at bedtime, his goodnight kiss seemed to be restrained. Her lips parted slightly, her heart thundering in her chest.

His lips grazed hers, and her knees weakened.

A cough nearby tore them apart. Miranda spun around at the sound, her cheeks flaming with embarrassment.

A tall, very overweight man waddled into the kitchen, letting the kitchen door swing shut behind him. "Don't mean to interrupt," he said.

"It's all right, Hollis," John replied, then introduced him to Miranda. "Hollis supplies me with pies every week," he said to Miranda.

"Got five of 'em in the wagon for you," Hollis said. "I'll go get them now."

After Hollis left, John reached into a cabinet near the back door and took out a metal box. Miranda's eyes widened as he set some money aside before putting the box back in the cabinet. Mentally, she calculated the cost of baking five pies compared to the amount lying on the counter.

John was being grossly overcharged. Anger bubbled up inside her.

Hollis came back into the kitchen with the pies and set them on the counter. "There you go, John. Three apple, a cherry and a blueberry, just like you ordered."

His smile widened as John counted out the bills into Hollis's pudgy hand. After a few comments about the weather, Hollis said goodbye to John, tipped his hat to Miranda, and walked out.

John was being ... swindled. She couldn't think of another word that fit better. And she couldn't let it go on one more day. John might be furious with her, but she was sure he'd see she was right eventually. "I'll be right back," she said, then hurried after Hollis.

Hollis was struggling to hoist himself into his wagon when Miranda called to him.

He paused, then lowered himself to the street. "Everything okay, Mrs. Weaver?"

She gave him a sweet smile. "Everything is just fine. I'm sure the pies you delivered are delicious, but we won't need you to supply the diner after today."

His brows lifted. She noticed his jaw tighten, but he made a good show of being concerned rather than angry. She'd give him that. "No? Mind if I ask why?"

"Now that John has married, there's no need to have someone else bake for the diner. I'm quite capable of taking care of it."

"Is that so?"

"It is. And to be honest, your pies are far too expensive," she said. "You make quite a profit on them."

"Well ... it's a lot of work ..."

Miranda let out a short laugh. "I've been baking pies since I was a young girl. I know exactly how long it takes and how much work it takes. I suspect you're charging the same amount from all your customers, which is far too much."

"And John agrees with you?"

For a few moments, guilt filled her, but she squashed it down. "He does now that I've explained it to him. He had no choice before. He does now."

"I see." He turned away and climbed into his wagon. Looking down at her, his face was flushed. "Then I'll bid you good day."

Miranda watched him drive off. Now she had to tell John what she'd done.

"You did what?" John slammed the lid on the soup pot on the stove and spun around to face Miranda. "Why in Heaven's name would you do that?"

Miranda's face paled and she took a step back. Was she afraid of him? Sure, he was angry, but there was no reason for her to flinch as if he was about to strike her. He'd never hit a woman in his life and he never would. Still, if the tone of his voice scared her, he'd have to make sure he changed it.

"I ... because he was overcharging you."

He wiped his hands on his apron and leaned back against the counter. "And what am I supposed to do now?"

She gave him a tremulous smile and his anger fizzled out like a wet match. Why couldn't he ever get angry with her?

"I'll bake the pies for you. You've tasted my pies. You told me they were better than the ones you served your customers here. Or was that just an empty compliment?"

"No ... they are better ..." he said. It was true. Her pies far outdid the ones Hollis made.

"And he was charging you far too much," she went on. "I can make three times as many pies for the same cost." She slid a glance around the kitchen. "Paper?"

"In the drawer."

She hurried across the kitchen and found the paper, then plucked a pencil out of his shirt pocket. As he watched, she tallied up the cost and slid the paper across the table toward him.

He looked down at her numbers and did a quick calculation of how much he'd paid Hollis every week since the diner opened. Hell, if these numbers were right, he would have been more than half way toward saving the money to expand the diner by now.

"Still," he said, his voice softening, "you don't have time—"

She crossed to stand close to him and put her hand on his forearm. "John, the girls will be going to school soon. I want to do this. I want to help you. This is one way I can."

He gazed down at her, breathing in her lavender scent, his gaze on the tiny freckles on her nose. How had he gotten so lucky? Not only was she pretty, she was kind and sweet and had accepted the girls like her own. And she was obviously a businesswoman, too.

And even more than any of that, he'd discovered he liked having her here working beside him.

"If we're going to have a real marriage, I need to be involved in everything that affects it. This diner isn't just your livelihood now. It's mine, too. I want to be involved. I want to help you to make it successful. You have to let me help you."

Nancy had never once wanted to have anything to do with the diner. She'd been quite content to take care of the house and the girls and leave everything else to him. As long as he provided for them, she was happy.

He didn't know quite how to deal with a woman who expected to be part of his business, but he had to admit it made him happy that she wanted to. Besides, one thing he'd learned since Miranda arrived was that he couldn't refuse her anything. And it seemed like this wasn't the time he was able to start.

CHAPTER 10

A week later, Miranda, Ellie and Hope hurried down the street toward the diner. Ruth's constant presence was taking its toll, and Miranda had realized the best way to deal with John's aunt was to stay out of her way before she said something she might regret.

Ruth was John's family, and as such deserved her respect, but every day it was getting harder and harder to bite her tongue. So she'd done the only thing she could think of to do.

Every morning, she'd hurried to help the girls to make their beds, and then she'd taken them out. Ruth wasn't pleased, but Miranda had stood her ground. She and the girls had taken long walks down by the river where Miranda had taught them about the birds who lived in the trees and the wildflowers that grew on the banks. They'd picked wild berries in the woods at the edge of town, and Miranda had shown them how to tell the animals by their tracks in the dirt.

And most days, they'd sat under the trees beside the river and Miranda had read to them.

She'd noticed a change in the girls. Hope was more talkative now, and even though she'd likely always be quieter than Ellie, she was much happier than she'd been when Miranda arrived.

Today, Miranda was going to teach them to bake apple pies at the diner. They were excited, and if she was being honest, she was excited to be able to spend the afternoon with John.

"Well, if it isn't my three favorite ladies," John said when they opened the kitchen door and went inside after lunch. Hope and Ellie immediately scrambled into the two chairs at the table.

Even though it was an off-hand comment, Miranda's heartbeat tripled. If only she truly *was* one of his favorite ladies ...

"I'd like to make the pies here today, if you don't mind," Miranda said, taking off her gloves and setting them on top of her reticule on the table.

John's brows lifted. "Really? Something wrong with the kitchen at home?"

Yes, Miranda wanted to say, *Ruth's in it*. Instead, she shook her head. "I thought it would be nice for us to work here with you. You have more room here, and I'd like to start teaching the girls how to bake."

"Then help yourself to whatever you need and I'll try not to get in your way."

Miranda met his gaze. Her insides buzzed. "You're never in my way," she murmured.

"When can we have pie?" Ellie asked, tugging at Miranda's skirt.

Miranda laughed. "We have to make the pastry first and put in the filling, and then they have to cook so the pastry turns golden brown."

"Then can we have pie?"

"After it cools, we'll have pie."

While Miranda prepared the pastry for the pies she'd promised to make for the diner, she also let the girls make their own pastry and roll it out. More pastry clung to the rolling pin than stayed on the floured surface, but the girls were having fun. She'd never heard them laugh so much, and it warmed her heart to think they were enjoying themselves the way little girls should.

"Mine's better than yours," Ellie said to Hope as she picked up a wad of pastry off the table and pressed it against the edge of the tin pie plate. "See?"

"No it isn't," Hope protested. "You got yours all messy. Mine isn't."

"Yeah, but you got holes in yours."

"So?"

"That's enough!" Miranda stood back from the table and planted her hands on her hips. "Ellie, there's no need to speak to Hope that way."

"But—"

"No buts," Miranda continued. "You and Hope are sisters, and you're so lucky to have each other."

"Do you got a sister?" Ellie asked.

A wave of grief washed over Miranda. Most of the time, she managed to tamp it down, and keeping herself busy with chores around the house helped. But there were times, especially when she woke before dawn and there was nothing but silence, when her sadness almost suffocated her.

How should she answer Ellie's question? She couldn't quite bring herself to say she didn't have a sister, almost as if Beth had never existed. Yet telling the girls about Beth's death might be distressing for them.

She slid a look in John's direction, the slight arch of her brows asking the unspoken question. He nodded slightly.

"I used to have a sister. She was the best sister I could have asked for."

Ellie's brows wrinkled. "Where is she now?"

Miranda's throat tightened. Oh, if only she could see her one more time ... "She's in Heaven."

"With Mama?" Hope asked. "Does she know Mama?"

Miranda caught a glimpse of John out of the corner of her eye. He'd stopped stirring the stew in the pot and was watching them.

Miranda smiled faintly. "Maybe. They might be friends now. I like to think so. Don't you?"

Hope nodded. "Like we are, right Ellie?"

"Uh huh."

Miranda plastered a smile on her lips. She didn't want the girls to dwell on sadness. "Now, we'd better get back to work. If we don't hurry and finish the pies, there won't be time to have a piece before supper."

John closed the ledger on his desk and leaned back in the chair, his gaze drifting to the other side of the room where Hope was sitting on the floor between Miranda's legs while Miranda brushed her hair. In the soft light of the lamp on the table beside her, Miranda's eyes sparkled and her face glowed. Ellie sat on the floor beside Hope, playing with her doll. Miranda had already brushed her hair and braided it for bed.

Life was good, he realized. When he'd lost Nancy, he'd thought he'd never be able to be happy again. But over the past few weeks, ever since Miranda had come into his life, he'd found himself smiling more and even laughing again.

She'd worked a miracle with the girls, too. The children he thought he'd lost when Nancy died were back, giggling and playing like they should – at least when Aunt Ruth wasn't there. He'd seen over and over again how quiet they were when his aunt was there and how they opened up and enjoyed being with Miranda when she wasn't.

He'd have to deal with it eventually, but how could he tell the woman who'd helped him so much that she was no longer needed?

"You and Ellie have such beautiful hair," Miranda said. "Every girl in school is going to be so jealous of you."

Ellie stopped brushing Rapunzel's hair and looked up at Miranda. "What if the other girls at school don't like us and don't want to be friends with us?"

Miranda smiled. "Of course they'll want to be friends with you. Why wouldn't they? You're beautiful, wonderful girls. You're kind and sweet and friendly. I bet by the time you get home tomorrow you'll have lots of new friends."

Hope twisted around to look up at Miranda. "But maybe the teacher won't like us—"

"If you're well-behaved and polite, just like I know you will be, your teacher will like you. I promise. Now let me finish braiding your hair and then you can go and get your nightgowns on for bed."

Fifteen minutes later, when Hope and Ellie were tucked into bed, John got up from the desk. "Are you sure that was wise?" he asked.

Miranda looked up from the sock she was darning. "What was?"

"Praising the girls so much," he said. "It is wise to praise them so much?"

Miranda frowned and wove her sewing needle into the sock and rested it on her lap. "You'd rather I criticize them?"

"Well ... no ..."

"Oh, just tell them their faults and that they aren't worth anything?"

"Now you're being ridiculous—"

"Am I?" Miranda interrupted.

John could tell by the sharp tone of her voice and the tension in her hands in her lap that he'd hit a sore spot. "Then obviously you didn't hear that when you were growing up."

"No, I didn't," he said. "I'm taking it that you did."

Miranda let out a breath. "Almost every day," she said. "I wasn't pretty enough, I wasn't tiny enough, I was clumsy, I was stupid. I'd never amount to anything. Shall I go on?"

John shook his head. "I'm sorry—"

"It wasn't that my mother didn't love me. I'm sure she did, and I'm sure she thought that by telling me what was wrong with me, I'd fix my faults." She let out a small laugh. "But some things were out of my control. I was never small and dainty like my sister and no matter how much I – or my mother – wanted me to be, it was impossible."

Being treated the way Miranda had been all her life, it was a wonder to John that she'd grown into such a sweet and caring woman.

"I want Hope and Ellie to grow up to be confident strong women, not women who aren't happy with themselves."

"If they get too full of themselves, they'll be insufferable and they'll never get husbands."

Miranda made a sign of a cross above her heart. "I won't let that happen."

John gazed at her, his heart swelling with emotion he was sure he'd never feel again. He cared about Miranda more than he'd allowed himself to admit, even to himself. She'd come into his life and taken him and his children as her own and treated them with nothing but kindness. And she'd brought light into the darkness that had overtaken them all.

"I won't," she repeated.

He smiled at her and nodded. It occurred to him suddenly that he trusted her. Completely. And if he wasn't real careful, he'd find himself falling in love with her, too. If he hadn't already …

Breakfast wasn't the leisurely meal it usually was the next morning. John had decided to open the diner a little later than usual so that he could see the girls off on their first day of school.

Miranda bustled about, realizing this would be the routine every morning now that the girls were going to school.

She glanced at the clock. The girls had to leave in ten minutes, and neither of them had finished eating. "Hurry, girls," she said. "You don't want to be late on your first day."

Ellie drained her milk and she was shoveling a mouthful of pancakes into her mouth when the door opened and Ruth marched in.

"Ellie!" Ruth spat out before she'd even taken her hat off. "What have I told you about stuffing food into your mouth?"

Ellie swallowed quickly. For a moment, Miranda was terrified Ellie would choke. Luckily, she didn't, and she hurried away before Ruth could say anything more. Miranda was annoyed. She shouldn't be, she supposed, but for some reason, she'd assumed that since the twins were going to school, Ruth wouldn't be stopping by. Whenever it had come up, Ruth had reasoned that she was helping to look after the girls. So why now? Miranda didn't need anyone to look after her.

She managed to keep quiet until the girls left for school, but as soon as the door closed behind them, she knew she couldn't hold her tongue a minute longer. She didn't want to get into a confrontation with Ruth, mostly because she knew she'd end up feeling terrible, but she'd been looking forward to having some time to herself, to taking care of her own home, and even going to the café to help John in the afternoons when she had time.

Now it seemed she'd never have a minute without Ruth's critical eyes on her.

"I'm surprised to see you this morning," she said to Ruth as she cleared the breakfast dishes from the table.

"Why?"

"Now that the girls are in school—"

"There's still work to be done here, and I doubt you can handle it all yourself."

Miranda bristled. "Before I married John, I was a housekeeper in a mansion back east. I do know how to clean a house."

"Were there no other maids?" Ruth asked, emphasizing the word *maids*. "Surely you didn't do everything."

"But I did," Miranda assured her. Yes, she was stretching the truth, but only a little. In the Tolliver house, she'd mainly been responsible for the fireplaces and the downstairs rooms, but cleaning was cleaning.

"Well then … it looks like I'm not wanted here any longer …"

Miranda struggled to contain the sigh that threatened to escape. Ruth knew exactly how to manipulate people. That much was plain to see. But Miranda was not going to be manipulated one second longer. "Of course you are," Miranda said, hoping God wouldn't strike her down for the lie. "And John and I appreciate everything you've done for him and the girls. You gave up so much to help him."

"That's true," Ruth agreed. "I gave up everything, and let me tell you, it was difficult. I had to sacrifice my work with the church, the Ladies' Society—"

"And I'm sure your friends miss you terribly."

Ruth nodded. "They do. Why, I haven't had luncheon with them in months."

Miranda plastered a gentle smile on her face. "Then you should take the time to enjoy yourself again. Without your help, I'll be much busier, but I'll be sure to let you know if I get too far behind in my chores."

"Well … I do miss my friends and my charity work. Why, just the other day, the Benevolent Society asked for my help …"

A few minutes later, the door closed behind Ruth and Miranda breathed a sigh of relief.

"Nicely done," John said with a grin.

"Thank you," she said, returning his smile. "Working for the Tollivers gave me plenty of practice smoothing ruffled feathers. They were the most unhappy family I've ever known."

"You almost made it sound like it was Aunt Ruth's idea."

"I hope so. Now, you'd better hurry yourself or your customers will be hammering at the door."

John bounded up and crossed to give her a quick peck before he left. "I'll see you tonight," he said, grabbing his hat off the hook behind the door.

"If I get my chores finished early, I'll come and help you if that's okay."

He paused and smiled. "I'd like that."

Miranda's heart swelled. He was growing to care for her. She knew it. If only she could figure out how to make him love her, her life would be perfect.

CHAPTER 11

The days flew by and Miranda settled into a routine. The weather was getting colder, and John had told her that soon, they would likely have snow.

Most days, as soon as the girls left for school in the morning, she hurried through her chores, prepared supper to be cooked later and spent the afternoons at the café working with John. Often, in the evenings, she'd take her needles and yarn out of the basket beside her chair and sit knitting quietly while John read or caught up on the accounting for the café.

She was happy … well, as happy as she could be without John's love. While she still had moments when grief overtook her, those times were becoming less and less, and even a few times she managed to think of her sister with a smile.

She still missed Lily, too, but she hoped that one day, she'd have a friend like her in Sapphire Springs. She was quickly becoming friends with Rosita and Poppy, but

125

even so, it wasn't the same as having a friend who'd known you since you were a young girl.

After discussing it with John, she'd written to Lily a month before and invited her to come to Texas, either for a visit or to stay.

Miranda hummed to herself as she hurried down the street toward the café. She'd stopped at the post office and found a reply. Unable to wait until she was home to read Lily's letter, she'd perched on the edge of the bench in front of the post office and ripped the envelope open.

Lily wrote that Mrs. Tolliver had found out she'd given Miranda the newspaper and fired her, too. Luckily, a new family had moved in nearby and she'd found another position almost immediately. She also wrote that if Miranda ever wanted to come back, there would be a position waiting for her.

Miranda had no desire to go back to Beckham. Other than her grief over losing her sister, she was happy. She loved her children, her new home, and her new husband.

She continued reading the letter, and excitement filled her when she read that Lily was planning to visit in the spring. Hopefully, she'd decide to stay and maybe even find a husband, too.

John looked up from the dough he was shaping and gave her a wide smile when she opened the door to the diner a few minutes later.

She knew John appreciated the help, and even though she'd never told him, she was happiest when she was with him. There was no question in her mind that what she felt for him was love. Not that she'd ever been in love before, but what else could it be? She wanted to spend every minute of her life with him. If only he felt the same way.

There had been times over the past few weeks that she'd caught him looking at her, a strange expression on his face. As soon as she met his gaze, though, he quickly looked away.

Was he sorry he'd married her? She couldn't help but wonder since he'd never made any advances toward her since their wedding night. Yes, he kissed her before he left the house in the morning and he kissed her goodnight, but those were nothing more than mere brushes of his lips against hers. He made sure no other part of him touched her in any way.

"I didn't expect to see you today," he commented, interrupting her thoughts. "Weren't you planning to visit with Poppy and Rosita?"

"Poppy's father-in-law is under the weather again, so she had to go out to his farm to take him something to eat, so we decided to postpone until tomorrow." She untied her bonnet and took her coat off, hanging them both on the hook beside the back door.

"Why he doesn't just move in with them is beyond me," John said, taking the tray of rolls and sliding them into the oven. "It would be a lot easier for Poppy and Tom to take care of him."

"It would," she agreed. "Now, I'll clear the tables and then I'll make a pot of chicken and dumplings if you like."

"I know my dinner customers would like that," he

said. "I think they've started coming more for your cooking than mine."

Miranda chuckled. "We each have our own dishes, and between the two of us, I think they're happy no matter who's cooking."

John wiped his hands on his apron, his gaze searing her. "We're good together, you and I."

Her breath stuck in her throat. Yes, they were good together in the café, and she was convinced they could be even better together, if only he didn't find her so unattractive.

Maybe if she was slim, like Poppy. Or prettier. Or …

An idea formed in her mind. She couldn't do anything to make herself prettier. Her hair was still a drab brown, her freckles still dotted her nose, and her features were still too large, in her opinion.

But she could do something about her weight. Would he love her if she was thinner? She didn't know, but it was worth trying.

Starting today, she decided, she'd stop eating so much, and if that's what it took for him to love her, she was willing to starve herself until she was thin enough that he'd want a real marriage.

Something wasn't right.

John cast a glance in Miranda's direction. For the past four days, Miranda had barely eaten anything at all. She still cooked their meals, but lately she had one excuse or another why she wasn't eating. Tonight, she'd told him she'd snacked so much while she was preparing the roast beef and vegetables that she was already full.

If she was sick … Memories flooded him. Nancy's illness had started the same way, with a loss of appetite and fatigue so severe she could barely get out of bed. Then came the pain, pain so excruciating that she'd pleaded with him to put her out of her misery. And then, finally, her suffering ended.

Was it possible …?

"Are you sick?" he asked. "Is that why you're not eating?"

She glanced up from the bowl of whipped cream she was setting on the table. "No. Not at all. I feel fine."

Something in her eyes told him she wasn't telling him the truth. But why would she lie? Unless she was trying to protect him? He'd talked to her about Nancy's illness, about how devastated he'd been watching her suffer and not being able to do anything about it. Was Miranda sick and she didn't want him to go through the worry again?

His insides twisted and his throat tightened. He couldn't lose another woman he loved.

The realization that he'd fallen in love with Miranda hit him so suddenly that he sucked in a breath and promptly choked on a pastry crumb.

"Lift your arms, Papa," Ellie commanded. "Like this." Through his tear-filled eyes, he saw Ellie raising her arms over her head.

He coughed and sputtered but did as he was told until finally the crumb dislodged itself from his throat.

"Are you all right?" Miranda asked, handing him a glass of water.

He nodded. "I'm fine," he said which was so far from the truth it was an outright lie.

He ate the rest of his pie in silence, then got up and crossed to the door. He took his hat off the hook and planted it on his head. "I need some fresh air," he said. "I won't be long."

Miranda frowned, but said nothing. He was glad of that. He didn't want to have to explain why he needed to get away. He needed to think, to make sense of the sudden revelation he'd had. And he needed to figure out what he was going to do about it.

Nothing had worked out the way he'd planned. He'd sent for a woman who could look after his home and raise his girls. Nothing more.

He'd loved Nancy deeply. He'd liked her, too, and they'd gotten along well, hardly ever having a disagreement.

But even though he didn't want to admit it, even to himself, he liked Miranda more than anybody he'd ever met, even Nancy. She worked harder than most men he knew and he'd never heard her complain. She had a ready smile and a kind word for everybody she met, and most of all, she made him feel that he could conquer the world if he had a mind to.

If he lost Miranda, too, he'd never survive it.

Miranda stood at the window and watched as John

disappeared around the corner. Where was he going? To the saloon? To find a woman?

She knew men had physical needs. Since he didn't come to her, she assumed he was going elsewhere to take care of those needs with another woman. He went out every Friday after supper. He was never gone more than an hour and when she'd asked where he went, all he told her was that he went for walks to get fresh air since he was indoors all week.

A lump of sadness clogged her throat. She was so hungry, and it seemed it would take weeks before she was thin enough to make him want her *that* way.

It had only been a few days, and it was torture to cook and bake for him and the children without eating most of it. All she'd allowed herself was enough to keep her alive and give her enough energy to still do her chores.

Her stomach grumbled.

Ellie came to stand beside her. "Why is there a noise coming from inside you? Did you eat too much? My tummy makes noises sometimes, too, and Aunt Ruth says it's because I eat too much."

Anger clawed at her. She'd sometimes wondered why Ellie seemed to pick at her food, rarely finishing what was on her plate. The little girl used up so much energy during the day that it had surprised her to see she didn't have a good appetite. Now she understood why, and it infuriated her.

She'd heard the same words from her mother more times than she could count, that she should curb her appetite, always "for her own good."

At the time she'd tried to eat less, but eventually she'd given up. Would she be slim enough now to make John want her if she'd listened to her mother? Possibly, but she wouldn't allow anyone to make Ellie feel that she needed to be thin to catch a husband.

Heavens, the girl was only five years old. She had years before she had to worry about what a man thought of her.

Miranda crouched to meet Ellie's gaze evenly. "My tummy rumbles when I don't eat enough. Maybe you could try to eat a little more and see if it stops."

"But Aunt Ruth—"

"Isn't here," Miranda interrupted. "It'll be our secret for now, okay?"

Ellie nodded, then scampered away.

Now all Miranda had to do was find a way for her own stomach to stop complaining about the lack of food.

It had been raining for two days, but finally the clouds had disappeared and the sun shone again. Miranda lifted the rag out of the bucket of vinegar water and wrung it out. The windows were filthy, and she'd set aside the entire afternoon to clean them. A pot of stew simmered on the stove inside, and two loaves of bread were rising on the worktable.

Miranda had barely started when she heard a squeak as the front gate opened behind her and a familiar voice called out. "Good afternoon, Miranda."

Miranda let out a sigh. Not today of all days. Still, she plastered a smile on her face and turned to face Ruth as she came up the walk toward her. "Good afternoon, Ruth," she said as pleasantly as she could manage. "On your way somewhere?"

"No," Ruth replied, setting her reticule on the rocking chair near the door. "I haven't looked in on you all for a few days and I wanted to see how you were faring without me?"

Miranda bristled. "We're doing fine, Ruth," she said. We haven't starved to death yet, she wanted to add.

"How are the girls?"

"They're out playing right now and likely won't be back for some time."

"I see."

"I'd offer you some tea, but the window is streaking. I need to finish —"

"You don't have enough vinegar in the water," Ruth put in, leaning over and sniffing loudly. "I always add plenty and the windows sparkle when I'm through."

"It's enough," Miranda contradicted. "I'm sure they'll be clean when I'm done. So if you'll excuse me—"

"It would have been wise to sweep the porch before you started," Ruth went on. "That way, any water that drips won't turn the dust to mud."

"I prefer to mop the floor when I'm done."

"Well … that's not the way I would do it …"

Miranda noticed her grip tightening on the rag and had to consciously loosen it. "That's the way I do it."

133

She turned away and while Ruth looked on, she ran the rag over the window in long strokes.

"You're welcome to come inside," she said when she was finished. Leaving the rag in the bucket, she opened the door and went inside. She held back a sigh when she heard Ruth's footsteps behind her.

"I'll make tea if you like," she offered.

Ruth sat down. "Yes, please."

She was just finishing up when Hope and Ellie raced into the house. While Hope's dress and hair were still clean and tidy, Ellie's hair had escaped her pigtails and her face and dress were streaked with mud.

"Look what we got," Ellie said, proudly holding out her hand to show Miranda the tiny tree toad in her mud-covered palm.

"Ellie!" Ruth's voice was sharp. "Where did you get that thing?"

"It was in the grass near the trees over there," she said, pointing to a stand of trees at the end of the street.

"Get rid of it this instant!"

Ellie's smile faded. Hope took a step backward. "But —" Ellie began.

Miranda dropped the rag into the bucket and sent a withering look in Ruth's direction. Then she crouched to Ellie's level. "It's a pretty toad," she said quietly, "but it probably misses its family—"

Ellie shrugged.

"You want to get warts?" Ruth's voice demanded.

"What's warts?" Ellie asked.

"Ugly bumps that will pop out all over your body?"

Miranda wasn't going to listen one second longer. "Ruth, I don't think—"

Ruth paid no attention to Miranda, her whole focus on the two little girls.

Ellie's eyes widened and she turned to her sister. Hope's chin was quivering, and her eyes were filling with tears.

"And look at you," Ruth went on, "covered in dirt and mud. Why can't you be more like Hope. How will you ever grow up to be a lady—?"

Miranda had had enough. "Ruth!"

Ruth turned to face her. "What is it, Miranda? How can you let them—?"

Miranda took in a slow steadying breath to control her temper. "We need to have a talk, Ruth," she said as calmly as she could manage, then turned to the girls. "Why don't you take the toad back where you found it? I'm sure its mama is looking for it."

Both girls nodded and hurried off.

"What is it Miranda?" Ruth asked once the girls were out of earshot. "Are you upset about something?"

Upset didn't come close to the anger that had been festering inside Miranda since the day she arrived. She'd tried. Lord knew she'd tried, but this was the last straw and it was time to settle things once and for all.

Growing up, Miranda hadn't been able to stand up for herself. In service in the Tolliver household, again she'd been treated as less than a person worthy of respect. Even here in Sapphire Springs, she'd allowed Ruth to make her feel as if she was lacking.

Until this moment, she'd never been strong enough

to stand up for herself, to announce to the world that she might not be slim and pretty and feminine, but no one had the right to treat her as less than a woman because of it.

But now, she had a reason. The children. *Her children!* It was up to her to protect them from people like her mother, like Ruth, and like other people who would look down on them or try to change them. As long as the girls grew into women who were kind and responsible, no one should make them feel inferior. Especially Ellie.

"I'm very upset."

Ruth frowned. "What is it, dear?" she asked. "You know you really should—"

"Stop!"

"Excuse me?"

"Just stop!"

"What …? How dare you speak to me that way!"

"You've given me no choice," Miranda began.

"I don't know what you mean—"

"I've tried to be a good wife to John, to be a good mother to the girls, and even to be a friend to you. I understand that it was difficult for you when I got here, and I'm sorry if you felt as if you were pushed aside. But since the day I arrived, you've criticized me, both to my face and behind my back …"

She paused as she noticed a flush seep into Ruth's cheeks.

"You didn't think I heard you, did you?"

"Why—"

"You belittle my efforts, no matter what I do. Believe me, I know how to make a bed properly and how to sweep a floor, yet you always found fault with every single thing I did. That I could put up with, even though I didn't like it. But when you criticize the girls—"

"I'm only trying to teach them. It's for their own good—"

Miranda ignored Ruth's comment. "I kept quiet out of respect for John, but I will not keep quiet any longer. I will not tolerate what you're doing to those little girls. I won't let you make Ellie feel inferior to Hope. They are two different people, and they should be allowed to be different. You will not compare them to each other. Ever."

"John's children—"

"They're *my* children now too."

"I don't have to stand here and listen to this."

"That's right," Miranda said. "You don't. You're welcome to leave any time. You're also welcome to come back and visit us at any time, but only if you can restrain yourself from criticizing or commenting on how I take care of the house or raise the girls."

Ruth snatched her reticule off the chair and marched toward the door. "We'll see what John has to say about the way you've spoken to me today."

Before Miranda had a chance to respond, Ruth threw the door open. It slammed against the wall as she stormed out.

Miranda leaned back against the counter, sucking in deep breaths. Her heart pounded in her ribs and her legs trembled so badly she was afraid they'd buckle beneath her. She'd never spoken to anyone that way before, and it still shocked her that the words she'd heard had come from her lips.

She was frustrated … and oh, so hungry. Too hungry to resist the plate of cookies on the counter beside her.

Snatching up one, she popped it into her mouth, letting out a groan of delight as the chocolate filled her mouth. She'd go back on her diet tomorrow. Right now, she needed the comfort only chocolate could bring.

Two more cookies, and finally, she straightened, wondering what John would have to say about the whole situation when he got home.

CHAPTER 12

"*W*ant to tell me what happened today?"
John asked later that night once Hope
and Ellie were asleep.

He'd heard Ruth's side of the to-do that had gone
earlier when she'd stormed into the café and started
railing about how rude and ungrateful Miranda was,
and how henpecked he was to let his wife speak to his
aunt that way.

According to Ruth, Miranda had practically
attacked her for no reason, and he'd do well to take her
in hand before she became a complete shrew.

John had promised his aunt he'd have a talk with
Miranda, but he was sure her version would be a whole
different story.

He'd noticed Miranda had been unusually quiet
during supper and she'd barely touched her meal. That
wasn't unusual these days, though, he mused. What she
was eating would barely keep a bird alive. He'd also

139

started to notice there was a pallor to her skin and that the sparkle in her eyes was gone.

Miranda glanced up from the sock she was darning. "I'm sorry, John. I tried, but I just couldn't stop myself. I'm sure she told you everything."

"One thing I've learned over the years is to listen to both sides of an issue before I form an opinion. I've heard Ruth's. I'd like to hear yours."

"Fine." Miranda laid the sock down in her lap and threaded the sewing needle through it. Then, clasping her hands and putting them on top of the sock, she told him what had happened. "John, if Ruth criticizes me, I can accept that. I don't like it, but I can deal with it." She let out a short laugh. "Heaven knows I'm used to it. But I can't sit by and watch her talk to the girls the way she does, especially Ellie.

"I was very much like Ellie growing up. I was bigger than most of the other girls my age. I had a … healthy appetite, and I preferred playing outside to working on embroidery and learning to speak French. Which I've never once had occasion to use, by the way."

John dragged the rocking chair he was sitting in across the floor to face Miranda. He sat down and reached out to take her hands in his, his understanding gaze meeting hers.

"I told you about it before, the night you criticized me for praising the girls so much."

"I wasn't criticizing—"

"Yes. You were. And I understand you don't want the girls to grow up to be vain. But I know what it's like to be on the receiving end of criticism every day. My mother compared me to my sister every day," she went on. "I should be slim like her. I should act like a lady like her. I should be smart like her. That no man would ever want me because I was too big, too fat, too ugly."

"You're not—"

"My sister was dainty, and pretty, and spoke with a melody in her voice," she interrupted.

"I'm sorry I never got to meet her," John said, giving her hands a gentle squeeze.

Miranda swallowed back the lump of grief settling in her throat. "I loved my sister, but I wasn't her. I couldn't be her, no matter how much I tried. The older I got, the more inferior I felt, as if I wasn't worth anything. I'd hoped that coming here would be a fresh start. But it wasn't. Ruth continued where my mother left off when she died."

"I'm sure she doesn't mean—"

"Of course not," she replied, unable to hide the sarcasm in her voice. "She's always just trying to help. And I've sat quietly and taken all her 'helpful' comments. But today ... today she started comparing Hope and Ellie. And when she asked Ellie why she couldn't be more like Hope, it brought back all those memories. I ... lost my temper."

John released her hands and leaned back in the chair, scrubbing his beard-stubbled chin with one hand.

He was shocked at what Miranda had told him. He knew she didn't have much confidence in herself, but he'd had no idea how her mother's words had hurt her. And he'd brought her here to deal with a woman who rarely had a good word to say to anyone.

He was well aware of his aunt found fault with everything and everyone. Hell, that was one of the main reasons he'd advertised for a bride in the first place. He'd seen for himself how her attitude was affecting his children.

Taking her hands in his, he brought Miranda to her feet and wrapped his arms around her, drawing her to him until her body pressed against his. Her lavender scent washed over him, her hair tickling his chin.

He lowered his head and kissed her gently. "I hate that you grew up feeling as if you weren't good enough."

"I don't want Hope and Ellie to ever feel that they're not good enough," Miranda said once John released her "Especially Ellie. I want her to grow up to be the woman she wants to be, not to try to be something she's not just to please a man. I'm sorry I upset your aunt, and I'm sorry if I've caused a rift between you but—"

"You were right to speak up, and if there's a rift, it's her doing. She did admit you told her she's still welcome here."

Miranda nodded. "But only if she curbs her criticism of me and the girls."

"I'll talk to her and make sure she understands that."

"Thank you. Now I'm going to get ready for bed."

John watched her walk away. She'd almost reached the bottom of the stairs when he called out to her. She stopped and turned to face him.

He closed the gap between them.

"What is it, John?" she asked. "What's wrong?"

Hell, Miranda was more than good enough. His love for her swelled inside him, and it was time he told her so. "In case you still think you're not good enough, I want to tell you that you are. You're more than good enough. In fact, you're perfect, especially for me, and I … I think I'm falling in love with you."

Miranda's eyes widened and he heard the sudden intake of her breath. "You are?"

He nodded. "Honestly, I don't want to, and I don't … can't offer you a real marriage——"

Miranda gently pressed a finger against his lips. "It's all right. It's enough that you care about me. I understand why you don't want to …" A flush tinged her cheeks. "Well … you know …"

"You do?"

She nodded. "Perhaps one day that will change, but for now, you've made me very happy."

Miranda sat gazing out the window as the first rays of sun cast a glow over the mountains in the distance. She'd barely slept, her emotions in a whirl. Life was almost perfect. Almost. He loved her, and the knowledge that a man cared for her made her feel as if she might burst with the joy inside her.

No, he didn't want a real marriage, and she understood why. But once she lost enough weight, surely that would change too. She was already starting to see that her dresses were looser than they used to be. Another few weeks might be enough.

Her body tingled at the realization that one day he might want her the way she'd heard other men want women. Not that she knew exactly what happened between a man and a woman. She'd heard it was painful and unpleasant, but somehow, she didn't believe that John would ever hurt her.

And once they had a real marriage, he wouldn't have any reason to go to the saloon to satisfy his needs. She'd take care of every one of them right here at home.

John looked on as Miranda ladled the chicken and dumplings into a bowl in the kitchen of the diner after the supper rush was over. She carried it carefully to the table, then set it down in front of Hope. Ellie already had hers and was blowing on the steaming liquid.

As she leaned over, John noticed how thin her arms were, barely skin over bone. Something was very wrong with his wife. She was losing weight so quickly that her work dresses hung loosely on her now. She didn't seem to be sick, though, not like Nancy was. But if she wasn't sick, why had she lost her appetite?

"It's very hot," Miranda said to Hope, "so you'll both have to wait a few minutes before you eat it. If you're very hungry, you may have a slice of bread and butter until your soup cools."

Straightening, she saw John watching her and gave him a smile. "Are you almost ready to go home?" she asked.

"I'll be another couple hours," he replied, "so there's

no point waiting for me. Once the girls are finished eating, you may as well take them home."

If he got the chance, he was going to talk to her when he got there. Whatever was causing her weight loss, he needed to know. He couldn't stand her having secrets from him, and no matter what was wrong, they'd face it together.

And it was time for him to tell Nancy he'd fallen in love with Miranda. He needed to explain to Nancy that he couldn't keep his promise and hope she understood.

Miranda slid the knife around the edge of the pie plate to cut off the extra pastry on the crust of the apple pie she was preparing a few days later, then put the knife aside and began crimping the edges together.

A gust of wind rattled the window. She glanced outside, taking note of the dark clouds in the sky and the raindrops on the glass.

She sighed. She'd hoped to do the wash, but now it would have to wait.

A timid knock at the door drew her attention. Who would be out and about when a storm was coming?

Quickly, she grabbed a towel and wiped the flour off her hands as she made her way to the door and opened it.

She was surprised to see Ruth standing on the porch, the strings of her reticule wrapped tightly around her clasped hands.

"Good morning, Miranda," Ruth said.

Suspicion wormed its way into Miranda's brain. Ruth sounded …different, even though he couldn't exactly say what it was about her voice that had changed since the last time they'd talked.

"Can I come in?" she asked.

Miranda held the door open and stepped aside. Ruth brushed past her, but didn't keep going into the parlor. Instead she waited until Miranda had closed the door behind her.

"Is something wrong?" Miranda asked. She couldn't imagine why Ruth would be visiting after the way she'd stormed out the last time they'd been together.

"No … nothing's wrong …"

"I'm surprised you're out in this weather," Miranda said.

Ruth slid a glance to the window as if she didn't know it was beginning to rain. "I'd like to speak to you if you aren't busy."

Miranda's brows lifted. What could she possibly have to say that Miranda wanted to hear?

She crossed the room to the sofa, expecting Ruth to follow. She didn't. Unusual, Miranda thought. Ruth never waited for an invitation to sit down. "What is it, Ruth?"

"I … John came to see me yesterday. He pointed out that I'd been a little … overbearing." She paused as if she was waiting for Miranda to contradict him. When she realized that wasn't going to happen, she continued. "I came because … I want to apologize."

Miranda couldn't have been more shocked if she'd heard the sky was falling. Still, she couldn't quite accept

Ruth's sudden change of heart without suspicion. "You do?"

Ruth's head bowed, but not before Miranda noticed the slight nod. "John and the girls are the only family I have and I love them dearly. I only want what's best for them."

"I know that—"

Thunder rumbled outside.

"John told me about your childhood, and why you feel so strongly about … things. He also pointed out how … rigid … I've become. After he left, I gave it a lot of thought and realized he's right. I've grown old and set in my ways." She let out a short chuckle. "As I've gotten older, it seems I've become my mother, something I swore I'd never do."

I certainly hope I don't turn into my mother, Miranda thought.

"So, I came to apologize for overstepping and I hope you can forgive me."

Miranda noticed a quiver in Ruth's voice, a sound she never thought she'd hear. She nodded and gave Ruth a small smile. It would take some time before Miranda could completely forgive her, but she was willing to try. "Would you like a cup of tea?" she asked. "I just made a batch of cookies, too."

"You might as well go on home now," John said the next Friday evening as the last of the customers left the diner. "I'll finish up here."

Miranda glanced over at him as she slid the dirty plates into the soapy water. She'd been working alongside him all afternoon. "Are you sure? Ruth is with the girls so I don't need to rush."

Ruth had asked if she could take Hope and Ellie back to her house after school and start teaching them to knit. Miranda had been hesitant, but in the past few days, she'd noticed a difference in how Ruth spoke to the girls, and they seemed more comfortable around her now.

She'd question them when they got home, but she was willing to give Ruth a chance. And it gave her a little more time alone with John.

"I'm sure," he repeated.

"When will you be home?" she asked.

"In a bit." He dried a skillet and hung it on the hook near the stove. "I have something to take care of."

"Your walk?" It was Friday, and she knew he always took a walk on Friday evening after he closed the diner.

He nodded. "I won't be late."

Miranda folded the towel and draped it over the rail nailed to the wall. She shouldn't ask, but didn't she have a right to know where her husband went? "John?"

"Hmm?"

"Where do you go on your walks?"

Was the sudden change in his expression just her imagination, or was it guilt?

"Around," he replied, turning his back on her and busying himself at the counter. "Why the questions? Don't you trust me?"

Did she? She honestly couldn't say she did.

She didn't answer. She wrapped her cape around her shoulders and picked up her reticule. "I'll see you at home."

Then she walked out. Coming from the heat in the diner's kitchen, the air outside made her shiver. She wouldn't be surprised if she woke the next morning to frost covering the ground.

She hurried down the boardwalk toward the house, but the closer she got, the slower she walked.

At the corner of the street, she stopped, turning to look back toward the diner.

She shouldn't do it. Shouldn't even think about it. It was wrong. But she couldn't help herself. She had to know where he went.

He hadn't said how long he'd be, but judging by the dirty dishes stacked on the worktable, he'd be at least a half hour. That would give her time to go home and get warmer clothes for what she was planning.

The light still glowed from inside the diner when she slid into the alley between the bank and the gunsmith's shop across the street from the diner. Finally, John turned off the last of the lamps and came outside, closing the door behind him and locking it.

Miranda's heartbeat thundered against her ribs. She shouldn't be here, hiding in the shadows, spying on her husband. If he caught her … No, she wouldn't think about that.

He didn't see her. Digging his hands into his jacket pockets, he walked in the opposite direction, toward the edge of town.

He disappeared around the side of a building, and

Miranda hurried along the boardwalk to try to see where he was going.

Just when she was about to pass the saloon, three men came outside. She recognized them as regular customers at the diner. If they saw her … Quickly, she ducked into the shadowed alleyway.

As she looked on, they strolled down the steps to where three horses were tied to the hitching post. Frustration filled her. Why didn't they get on their horses and ride away? How was she supposed to find out where John had gone without the men seeing her?

The men talked for what seemed like hours before they finally went on their way. With a sigh of relief, Miranda peeked out of the alley. She was too late.

John appeared from behind the building and walked down the boardwalk. He stopped in front of the saloon for a few seconds, then went inside.

Miranda's chest tightened. Her throat squeezed shut and tears filled her eyes, spilling down her cheeks.

John had told her he was falling in love with her, and she'd thought once she lost weight, he would find her attractive.

But he didn't. He still found it necessary to go to the saloon and find a woman. She'd never have a real marriage, never have children of her own.

She could go back to Beckham, but how could she bear to leave Hope and Ellie?

CHAPTER 13

*M*iranda took a large spoonful of apple pie and whipped cream and put it into her mouth. Tears dripped onto the table, but she didn't care. She'd starved herself for nothing.

And as she'd trudged home after seeing John go into the saloon, it had occurred to her that she'd been doing the one thing she'd been determined not to do to the children.

She wanted them to grow up to be themselves, not to try to be something they weren't so they'd be accepted and loved. Yet wasn't that what she'd been doing? Trying to lose weight so that John would want her, that they could have a real marriage and maybe even more children one day?

She could never be a slim, feminine woman, yet until now she'd never truly accepted that. But now, she had no choice. She couldn't spend the rest of her life trying to be something she wasn't.

And if John couldn't love her because of her appear-

151

ance, there was nothing she could do about it. She wouldn't try any longer.

Ruth and the children had arrived shortly after she reached the house, and within a few minutes, they were safely tucked into bed and were sound asleep.

Her heart splintered at the thought of leaving them. She couldn't do it, no matter how hurt she was by John's rejection. His words of love meant nothing to him.

She sniffled as she took another bite of the pie, relishing the sweet taste as the apple mixture slid across her tongue.

She heard the front door open, and for a brief moment, she thought about hurrying upstairs so she wouldn't have to speak to him. But the moment passed. It was time to let him know exactly how she felt.

Her heart pounded in her chest as she rose from the table and took in a few calming breaths. Then she walked slowly toward the front door where he was hanging his jacket on the hook.

"The girls in bed?" he asked, turning to give her a smile.

Her pain faded, and anger took its place. He had the nerve to smile at her as if he'd done nothing wrong?

"Yes."

He hung his hat on the same hook, then turned to face her. A frown creased his forehead. "What's wrong? Are you all right?"

This was it! "No. I'm not all right."

He was beside her in an instant. "What is it? Are you sick? Hurt?"

"No. Yes—"

"Which is it?"

"Where did you go tonight?"

"You know where I went," he said quietly.

"Yes, I do. The saloon."

"Among other places."

Miranda didn't have any idea where those other places were since she hadn't been able to follow him when he disappeared behind the building. What was important, though, was that he'd gone to the saloon, and he was quite willing to admit it.

Her stomach churned, but whether it was pain or anger, she couldn't tell. "You tell me you're falling in love with me, but you go to the saloon to take care of your ..." Her voice lowered to a whisper. "Your physical needs. Or do you take care of them elsewhere, like somewhere at the other end of town?"

"What are you talking about?"

The tears welled up again, which infuriated her. "I saw you."

"Where?"

"I followed you when you went for your walk," she said. "Where did you go besides the saloon? To another woman's house maybe?"

"I'll tell you, but first you have to tell me why you're so upset."

Miranda fisted her hands and dug them into the small pockets on her flowered apron. "I came to Texas to be a wife and mother. I love Hope and Ellie as if they were my own daughters, and I hoped that eventually we might have a real marriage. On our wedding night, I saw how repulsed you were by me—"

"Repulsed? What the devil are you talking about? I wasn't repulsed by you—"

"Let me finish."

John raised his hands in surrender. "Go ahead."

"I know a man has needs. When you turned away from me, I knew then that you would find someone else to take care of those needs, and I understood that. Then I … I fell in love with you … and I didn't want you to go to anyone else."

"You fell in love with me?"

"I tried not to. I didn't want to, but I did. And I thought if I stopped eating so much, I'd lose weight and then … then you might stop going to someone else. That you'd want me instead."

He closed the gap between them and gripped her shoulders. "Are you telling me you were starving yourself deliberately so you'd be thinner?"

His jaw was tense, as if he was angry with her. What did he have to be angry about? She nodded.

"Are you crazy? Do you realize you scared me half to death? I thought you were sick, that I was going to lose you, too."

"I'm not sick, just sick and tired of trying to be the kind of woman a man is attracted to. I've lost weight. I'm thinner now, and yet you still go to the saloon."

"I went to the saloon to talk to Pete about helping me expand the diner."

Had she heard him right? "Really?"

He grinned. "I don't go to the saloon, Miranda. At least not for what you think."

"Where did you go earlier then?" she asked. "I saw you go behind the buildings at the edge of town."

"The same place I've been going every Friday, to the cemetery to talk to Nancy."

Miranda's heart sank, lodging in her stomach. Just when she thought there might be a future for them, he snatched it away.

"But tonight, I went to tell her I love my new bride, and I want to have a real marriage. I'd promised her I'd never love another woman. I was wrong. I think she understands, and I think she's happy that I found another woman I could love and who loved me and her children so much."

Miranda held her breath, afraid to let hope creep in. "You were at the cemetery?" she murmured, gazing into his dark eyes.

"I was. I loved Nancy, and she'll always have a piece of my heart. We were young, she was my first love, and she was the mother of my children. What I feel for you is a different kind of love, but it's stronger, deeper and so much more than what I felt for her."

Miranda couldn't believe what she was hearing. He loved her. He really did love her. She understood his feelings for his wife, and she respected that. If she was being honest, she would have thought less of him if he didn't have feelings toward the woman he'd once loved and lost.

"That's why you kissed me on our wedding night and then turned away? Because of the promise, not because you couldn't stand to touch me?"

He released her shoulders and cupped her chin in

one palm. Leaning down, he kissed her soundly until she was breathless when he finally raised his head.

"You really don't see how beautiful you are, do you?" he asked.

She shook her head.

Wrapping his hand around hers, he turned away, taking her with him as he crossed the room and led her up the stairs to their bedroom.

He stood aside at the door and gestured for her to go inside. He followed, closing the door behind him and ushered her toward the full-length mirror in the corner of the room.

"John? What are you doing? Why are we standing here?"

He came up behind her and wrapped his arms around her waist. "Look in the mirror," he ordered.

"Why? What—?"

"What do you see?"

"This is silly—"

"Tell me."

She stared at her reflection, her gaze sliding from her hair down to her feet. "I see a woman who's past her prime, whose hair is the color of mud and frizzes when it's damp."

"What else?"

"A woman whose facial features are too big, and whose body won't ever be dainty and slim no matter how tight her corsets are."

"You really see yourself that way?"

She nodded.

"Now let me tell you what I see," he said. "I see a

woman whose hair reminds me of the heat of fire, whose eyes sparkle with joy and are barely big enough to contain the love I see in them for me and our girls. I see a woman whose mouth is wide to hold the smiles and laughter she fills our home with, and whose body fits perfectly against mine. I see the woman I love. The woman I intend to love for the rest of my life."

Miranda's tears spilled over and trickled down her cheeks, but this time they were tears of happiness. Her love for John and their children filled her to overflowing.

"And we're going to have a real marriage?" she asked.

He grinned, a wicked look in his eye. "Oh, Mrs. Weaver, you have no idea," he went on, turning her to face him and reaching for the top button of her work-dress, "Now, let me show you how much I really do love you. All of you. Forever and always."

EPILOGUE

Ten months later

John wrapped an arm around Miranda's shoulder as they stood with the children and watched with a growing crowd of people as two men hung a banner above the Blue Sapphire announcing the grand re-opening.

Pride filled John, although he knew none of it would have been possible without Miranda's hard work. Soon she'd be too busy to help, he thought, sliding a glance at the small bump on Miranda's stomach where her hand was resting, even though she assured him she'd find time to still bake the pies the diner's customers raved about.

He looked around at his friends, his neighbors, all gathering to help him celebrate the expansion, and his chest filled with gratitude and love for the woman standing beside him. "I couldn't have done this without you," he told her.

Miranda grinned up at him. "We did it together."

"When Nancy died, I thought my life was over, that I'd never be happy again. How wrong I was. I've never been happier than I am right at this moment."

Not only had Miranda come to him and given herself to him and the girls without reservation, she had brought laughter and joy back into their lives and had done everything she could to help him realize his dreams.

Hector Delacruz and his daughters strolled up and stopped at his side. He tipped his hat to Miranda. "Congratulations," he said. "I wish you both much success. My daughters and I look forward to trying some of the new dishes you are offering now."

John smiled. "You won't be disappointed, Hector."

With a nod, Hector and his daughters moved on.

"Mama." Hope looked up at Miranda. "When can we go look for ribbons?"

"John, do you mind if we leave for a few minutes?"

John shook his head. "Take all the time you need."

Miranda and the children strolled off. A few seconds later, John heard another familiar voice and felt a hand give him a friendly slap on the back.

John looked behind him

Pete was standing there looking at the banner. "You really did it," he said. "Did you ever think the mail could bring you more than just a letter?"

John shook his head. "I surely didn't," he replied, his gaze watching Miranda and the girls disappear into the mercantile. "The mail brought me everything I ever dreamed of."

And, he thought, so much more.

MIRANDA

Keep reading for a preview of

MAIL-ORDER BRIDES OF SAPPHIRE SPRINGS: AUDRA

by Margery Scott

CHAPTER 1

Sapphire Springs, Texas

*N*eall Gardiner sat astride Apollo, his coal-black stallion, and surveyed the valley.

His valley.

The land was his, from the river that wound its way through the land a few hundred acres behind him to the emerald green grassland that rose into the foothills at the base of the Blue Mountains in the distance.

He smiled. He'd done well, and he was proud of what he'd accomplished in the past six years since his father died. He'd gambled, risked more money than he should have when he'd bought the steers from Abe Littlejohn to start his herd, but it had paid off.

Now, he had a reputation of raising some of the highest quality beef in the state.

He'd bought up the last thousand acres just the year

before, and he'd be adding another two thousand or so next month when Abe sold out to him and went to live with his daughter in Austin.

He had the perfect life. Well, almost perfect. That empty, gnawing part of him begged for something more. Something he'd had growing up, but had lost, little by little, ever since his father died. A family.

He'd always figured he'd be married by now, but he'd been so busy with the ranch that time had slipped by without him really even noticing. Now, with his thirtieth birthday approaching, it was past time to find himself a bride.

There were unmarried women in Sapphire Springs. Plenty of them, as a matter of fact, and more than a few who'd be willing to marry him. But how could he know which ones cared about him and which ones were only interested in the financial security and luxury he could offer? After what had happened to his cousin up in Fort Worth—the woman who'd supposedly loved him had spent every cent he'd had and more then ran off with a banker from somewhere in California—Neall was afraid to take the chance the same thing would happen to him. If he lost his ranch because of a woman …

There was one way to be sure the woman he married wanted him and not his money, he thought, turning Apollo in the direction of the ranch house. He flicked the reins, and the stallion set off at a trot across the field. He could marry a woman who didn't know him, a woman who'd know nothing about him other than what he told her.

He could get himself a mail-order bride.

It had worked for John Weaver, Neall reasoned. After John's wife died, he'd been left with a diner to run and two little girls to raise with nobody to help him except his aunt. John had sent away for a mail-order bride. He'd married Miranda the day she arrived. They'd had their own issues to deal with, but they'd worked it out and he was a happy man now.

Maybe Neall would be just as lucky. It was a gamble, but he'd never been afraid to take a risk when the reward was worth it.

As he rode closer, the ranch house came into view, large and impressive. He could see his whole family history in the construction of it—the original two-story house his great-grandfather had built when he and his great-grandmother had arrived in Texas from the Scottish lowlands with a dream and a few dollars to buy a parcel of land, the rooms added on when his grandparents had married, the addition his father had built when Neall was a baby.

Neall lived alone in that house now, except for Mrs. Davey, the housekeeper who'd looked after him since he was a boy. They might not be related by blood, but she was the only family he had left.

Apollo stopped at the bottom of the steps leading to the front porch. As Neall dismounted, his foreman, Tucker Gates, opened the front door.

"Afternoon, boss," Tucker said, coming down the stairs and approaching Neall. "I'll take Apollo to the barn and rub him down. I'm heading that way anyway."

"Thanks, Tucker."

Tucker took the horse's reins from Neall. "Left some bills on your desk for you to look over," he said.

"I'll do that," Neall replied.

Tucker ran his hand down Apollo's neck and took a few steps toward the barn before Neall called out to him. "I'm going into town later. Are you expecting any deliveries or need anything at the mercantile?"

"I can send one of the boys—"

"No need," Neall insisted. He'd never been a man to expect anyone else to do something he wouldn't do himself, and if he was being completely honest, he enjoyed working alongside his men, getting his hands dirty, feeling his muscles burn from a hard day's work.

"Got an order at the mercantile if you feel like taking the wagon," Tucker said.

"I'll do that."

Tucker nodded, then continued on his way with Apollo.

Neall climbed the stairs and went into the house, the smell of wood polish filling his nose. Mrs. Davey appeared in the doorway of the small room he used as an office. He'd always loved that room because of the huge windows giving him a view of the river and the cattle grazing in the fields. It used to be a receiving parlor, but he'd taken it over after his mother passed on two years before.

"I'm just finishing cleaning," she said, the faint Scottish burr she'd never been able to lose creeping into her voice. "'Course it would be a lot easier if you'd keep it tidy."

"Yes, ma'am, I will," he replied with a smile. His

messiness had been a bone of contention between them since he was a boy. He'd never outgrown it, and she'd finally given up trying to change his ways. Now, it was a shared joke between them. She complained; he agreed to do better.

"I've made a decision," he told her, changing the subject.

"Oh?"

"Yes, and since it'll affect you, too, I want you to hear it first."

A worried frown appeared between her brows. She twisted the dustrag between her hands until Neall grinned. "I'm getting married."

Mrs. Davey's brows shot up. "What?"

"Yes," he repeated. "It's time, don't you think?"

"Well past time if you ask me," she responded, a broad smile sweeping across her face. "Might I ask who the lucky woman is?"

His grin widened. "Well … I'm not sure yet, but as soon as I find out, you'll be the first to know."

VIP READER GROUP

Join Margery in her private reader group on Facebook for games, contests and conversation about books and life … and to help her when she gets stuck (which happens more often than she'd like.) Margery's group is always the first to hear breaking news and get exclusives nobody else gets. Come and join us!

www.facebook.com/groups/margeryscott

Margery Scott is the author of more than twenty-five novels, novellas and short stories in various genres. Although she grew up as far away from the old west as possible, Margery has always admired the men and women who settled the untamed land west of the Mississippi. Glued to TV westerns like Maverick, Rawhide and Gunsmoke, and reading stories of Annie Oakley, Roy Rogers and Rin Tin Tin, it was only natural that when she started writing, she wrote what she loved to watch and read. She now lives on a lake in Canada with her husband, and when she's not writing or travelling in search of the perfect setting for her next novel, you can usually find her wielding a pair of knitting needles or a pool cue.

Website: www.margeryscott.com
Email: margery@margeryscott.com

Follow Margery on:
Facebook: www.facebook.com/AuthorMargeryScott
Twitter: www.twitter.com/margeryscott
Bookbub: www.bookbub.com/authors/margery-scott
Instagram: www.instagram.com/margeryscott48

Made in the USA
Monee, IL
07 April 2020